NUNS WITH GUNS

A HOLIDAY CAPER

JAN JOHNSON

FARMHOUSE
PUBLISHING

ISBN: 979-8-9991399-3-1

INTRODUCTION

This Christmas, peace on earth is optional—but chaos is guaranteed.

When the well-meaning (and wildly unprepared) Sisters of Mercy have their van stolen by a man in bunny slippers, their quiet holiday plans skid straight into criminal mayhem. Suddenly, the sisters are tangled up with a crew of ex-cons, a rival gang with a grudge, and a dead body no one can quite explain—especially not the one in the basement.

At the center of the storm is Hope House, run by the earnest Brother Ben, a safe haven for displaced Ukrainian children seeking refuge from war. As tensions rise and old vendettas reignite, the sisters find themselves doing the unthinkable: picking sides, dodging danger, and wielding faith with a surprisingly firm trigger finger.

There is just enough Christmas spirit to remind everyone that mercy sometimes comes with backup. Equal parts heart, humor, and holy havoc, this is one yuletide you won't soon forget.

ALSO BY JAN JOHNSON

Mercy Series

My Heart's for You

Windows of My Heart

The Way to My Heart

Memoir

I Will Enter His Gates,

A Walk with God

Bible Study

Discovering Your Journey:

Finding God in Every Step

Christmas

Mistletoe @ Christmas Tree Lodge

Nuns with Guns

Books available in audio, print, and ebook

1

THE ONLY THOUGHT SWIRLING around in his head the week Bernardo Sanchez was released from his two-year stint in the clink was to see his daughter Amelia. She had been three when he was convicted of stealing an assault rifle from an FBI car. The thought of those irresistible dimples he liked to kiss, and soft curly brown hair he combed after her bath, made him smile. The thought of what he had missed during those two long years wiped the smile off his face.

His wife wasn't too happy about his jail time and didn't come to visit him or let him see Amelia. Not that he blamed her. Marie hadn't met him outside when he was released, and he wasn't looking forward to seeing her reaction to him showing up at their door. Maybe he'd be able to convince her he'd changed. And he had, hadn't he? He had gone through counseling and was going to start fresh. Get a job. An actual job with a real paycheck. Be able to support Marie and their daughter, Amelia. He could do this. She was a good woman and deserved his best. It was a worthy goal, for sure.

He knocked, and through the door was surprised to hear little footsteps. His chest swelled at the thought of laying eyes on his daughter. The door slid open, and she stopped still, looking up at him, expressionless. Her deep chocolate eyes stared at him —her curly hair pulled into a long pony. She looked just like her mama. Marie came up behind her, wrapped her arm protectively around Amelia's waist and pulled her in.

"What are *you* doing here?" Marie's eyes narrowed.

"I'm out. I wanted to see you and Amelia."

Marie rolled her deep brown eyes, the same ones he used to gaze into before... It made him want to pull her in and kiss her.

"Two excruciating years without a word. You left me to single parent and manage a full-time job to make up what income you didn't bring in." Her voice was rising. "And now you want to waltz in here and disrupt our lives? I don't think that's a good idea." She released Amelia. "Go sit on the couch and finish watching your show, Baby."

Bernardo watched his daughter run to the worn couch, pause to look at him, and jump onto it.

"I just want to talk to you. I don't expect you to welcome me, but could you just hear me out?"

Marie reluctantly moved aside and motioned with her head to the kitchen table. The kitchen was spotless. Dishes were put away, and the table was wiped. The floor was swept, and the shine reflected the overhead light.

Bernardo sat on the wooden chair and placed his hands under his thighs. "You never came to visit me."

"I thought it would be better for Amelia not to see the inside of a jail."

"But *you* could have come."

She shook her head. She set the kettle on the stove and turned up the gas, so the flames licked the kettle.

"Listen, I'm sorry." His hands started moving with his words. "What I did was really stupid. But that was two years ago. I've changed. I'm not the same man."

"And how am I supposed to know that? You're gonna have to build some trust here, you know."

"I know." He reached for her hand, and she pulled it away.

"Tell me about Amelia. Is she in school?"

"Yeah. Kindergarten."

"Does she like her teacher? Does she have friends?"

"She does." The teapot whistled, and she shut off the gas. "Tea?"

"Sure."

"You still like that licorice flavor?" She opened a drawer that contained several boxes.

"You remember that?" He watched her pour the water over the bag and hand him the cup, the one that said *I love my dad.* His eyes grew misty.

"Babe, I'd do anything to repair the damage I've caused. Leaving you to manage alone and not helping with the bills." He lowered his head.

She set the tea before him and sat. He wrapped his hands around the mug and slowly breathed in the fragrant steam.

She took a sip and said, "There's something you need to know. Amelia has a medical condition. The doctors have done extensive tests. She needs expensive medication that I can't afford, and state health insurance isn't going to cover it." A tear spilled down her cheek. Her eyes caught his. "She's gonna die, Bernardo."

———

THAT HAD BEEN two weeks ago. Marie had allowed him to spend some time with Amelia. He'd spent a day with her at school, taken her for ice cream, and a movie—not all on one day. She wore out easily. Marie hadn't been ready to let him move back in, so he'd resorted to couch hopping. Not ideal, but better than living in his jeep, or worse yet, sleeping on the sidewalk.

JOEY LAGRATTO SWIPED a hand down his tattooed face, his eyes closed and let it rest there as he whooshed a long breath. Getting caught and landing in jail were risks of pulling a heist. It had put him back a spell. But now that he was out, he just had to figure out the next step. He reached for his phone and tapped in a few numbers.

"Bernardo, I need you to take care of an item for me while we're out of commission. Meet me at four."

"What's in it for me?"

"Don't worry, you'll get your fair share."

BERNARDO'S SHOULDERS TENSED. He didn't like being in a position of having to submit to Joey. But for now, he felt like he had no choice. He'd been spending more time couch surfing at his house than anywhere else, along with the five others who had been in jail with Joey. There was always a price to pay.

Bernardo nervously tossed a Rubik's cube up and down. What was so important about a silly little kid's toy? When Joey had tossed it to him, he gave Bernardo a look that said he better protect it with his life. Did it hold gold or something? Knowing Joey there was something more valuable than gold.

Bernardo slid into his navy green jeep, the paint faded through to the base, and coughed the engine to life, leaving a trail of exhaust fumes in its wake. Weaving between cars on the D.C. highway, he thought of how his reward would be enough to get him on his feet. No more couch hopping or digging in the garbage cans for his next meal. His hands tightened on the steering wheel.

A glance in the mirror showed someone tailing him. He tested it out, turning at the next exit and into an old neighborhood, swerving into the left lane, and passing a semi-truck. No doubt about it—he was being pursued.

Bernardo parked the jeep in a one-way alley and jumped out. He slid the Rubik's Cube into his sweatshirt pocket and exited on the other side. Walking nonchalantly along the sidewalk, he was not aware that he was wearing the bunny slippers he had run out of the house with. He slid a glance back. No one was going to keep him from this job. It had to end in success.

2

It was just your regular average day—get up at six, say morning prayers, eat breakfast. Breakfast was anything but ordinary since nuns only have what is donated to them. It breeds creativity for those on kitchen duty, for sure. Take this morning, for instance. They were out of cereal. Out of pancake mix. There was flour, but no baking powder or eggs. But there were leftover mashed potatoes and gravy, cheddar cheese and a box of prunes. They learned quickly to enjoy and be thankful for whatever blessings God sent their way.

Breakfast was over, and Mother Joanna led the six nuns to daily mass in the little chapel attached to their convent. Fr. David had been their celebrant for as long as she could remember, and Mama J was pushing forty. He kept the homily short and to the point. They were encouraged to feed the hungry, give clothing to the poor, take care of orphans. The uszh.

Mama J rounded up the crew to give directions for the day.

"We're headed to downtown D.C. to donate food to the Rescue Mission, and we'll stay and serve meals. Sisters Ignacia and Irene will remain here to cook and clean. We should be home by dinner."

Following the others down the ten cement steps to the van, Mama J stopped to cross herself as she passed the statue of Jesus, their provider, protector, and director of their paths. Sister Edith had the van hood up, pouring a quart of oil into the engine. She twisted the cap. The hinges creaked as she shoved the hood into place. That girl kept them in excellent hands. There wasn't anything she couldn't fix.

Sister Agnes used both chubby hands to shove the squeaky sliding door shut, and they were off. It was an uncharacteristically warm September day.

Mama J wiped beads of sweat with a hanky and slid into the driver's seat. She had been telling their general superior for years that they should have lighter-weight habits as options. She was told that they should humble themselves and learn to be happy in all circumstances. Perhaps that's why they wore a coif —to soak up the droplets God so generously designed to cool them down.

"Mother Mary Joanna, will we be visiting the orphans today as well?" Sister Edith cranked the handle to roll down the window where hot, humid air blew in, causing sweat to trickle under her armpits.

"These kids are not orphans," Sister Ignacia. "They still have parents. They're displaced children." Her voice was bold but not disparaging.

"No, we won't have enough time. We can schedule them in tomorrow." Mama J turned on the blinker to take the exit.

"Oh good! I just love being with the children. They're so full of energy. I've been finding more games that we can play with them—cribbage and dominoes," Sr. Irene said.

Sr. Edith leaned against the front seat. "Mother, are we going to collect Christmas gifts for them? Maybe we could get them some Lego, or an Erector set."

"Yes, of course. In fact, Fr. David has a bag of toys from the rectory. I'll stop by and pick them up."

Sister Agnes fanned herself with an accordion-pleated piece of paper, her round cheeks red, dripping with sweat.

"It's just so sad that they had to be removed from their parents. I know they're safer here, away from the war, but still..."

"It just gives us another opportunity to offer compassion, my dears. Hands and feet of Jesus."

Mother Joanna stopped at the rectory to pick up the bag of toys. She placed them in the front seat of the van and drove to the Mission, where she found a parking spot directly in front. A few haggard men leaned against the brick wall, one wearing a DARE t-shirt and a skirt, another with camo pants and a tank top. They jumped from their spots and ran to help unload crates of canned tomato soup, spaghetti-o's, fresh salad fixings, and loaves of bread and butter.

"How you doin', Mama J?" Angelo's black dreads bounced as he grabbed a box.

"I'm well. And you Angelo? Were you able to get that sore tooth taken care of?"

"Yeah, thank you for lining me up wi' dat dentist van. You da best!" He slapped her on the shoulder—an action that had taken her some time getting used to.

Mateo, wearing a backward baseball cap, grabbed another crate. Mama J shut the tailgate, and they followed him inside to the kitchen, where delicious smells of fried onions and garlic emanated.

"There's been a couple of guys hanging out here lately. New ones. Never seen them before. They seem a little shifty. Be careful." Mateo lifted his cap and swiped the sweat off his forehead with the back of his hand.

Mama J wasn't worried about shifty. She'd been in a lot of shady neighborhoods. God always came through with the hand of mercy on her every time. She shrugged. God looks at the heart, not the appearance of men, right?

———

"Is it okay if we wait in the van for you? Everything's cleaned up." Mother Joanna nodded at Sister Agnes.

"I'll be there soon. I just need to talk to someone."

Sr. Agnes climbed into the passenger side while Sisters Edith and Teresa took the back seats. She levered the seat back to accommodate her long legs. They left the doors open, hoping to let in a breeze.

"Hey, look at this guy walking down the street. Does he look alright to you?" Edith said. They leaned forward and watched where she pointed.

"He's wearing bunny slippers. Perhaps we could find him some new shoes. It looks like he wears size eleven," Sr. Teresa said.

"He's glancing behind him." Edith wrung her hands.

"And walking faster." Teresa said.

"There's a cop following him. Should we be worried?" Edith scrunched up her shoulders.

Irene put her hand on Edith's shoulder. "Look—he ducked between the cars. I'm sure the cop will take care of him."

"He's running towards us! Oh, no!" Edith screamed as Bunny Slippers jumped into the driver's seat and reached for the keys. The police officer thrust his arm through the window and tried to wrestle the keys from him, without success.

"Get out of the van. Everybody out. Now!" Sister Teresa took charge. They tumbled onto the sidewalk, one after the other, like piles of puppies.

"Just let him go," the officer said. "You'll be better off."

They heard whoops and hollers as Bunny Slippers took off —his fist raised in triumph.

Sister Teresa patted her pockets. "Oh no, we left the cell in the van. Officer, may I borrow your phone?"

He handed his to Sr. Teresa who punched in the numbers.

"Hello? This is Sr. Teresa. Who is this, please?"

"Tony."

Her face scrunched into a puzzle. "Hi, um, Tony. Can I ask if you're driving a grey van?"

"Nope. Some guy just threw this phone outta the window of a van, so I picked it up."

"I see. Well, that guy stole our van, and we're in front of the Rescue Mission, and we have no way to get home. Do you think you could return our phone so we can let the others know what happened?"

"Well, aren't you in luck, Lady? Six years ago, I would have sold it to buy drugs. Six months ago, I would have kept it. But today's your lucky day. I'm gonna be nice and return it. I'll take the bus and be there soon."

"Bless you!" She handed the phone back to Officer Bradley.

Sr. Teresa rounded up the others in a circle where they spread their arms around each other and proceeded to pray. Obviously, this was a situation they would need to surrender.

"OKAY GIRLS, I'm ready to go." Mother A walked out of the mission, ready to return to the convent. She paused.

"And please bless Mr. Bunny Slippers because I'm sure he doesn't know what he's doing," Sr. Teresa finished.

"Where's the van? Did you move it?" It had been parked in front of the Mission. Mama J did a double take.

"Ummm," Sr. Teresa began.

"So, there was this guy—" Sr. Edith.

Size eleven, I think." Sr. Irene.

Sr. Edith spilled out the words. "He got in the van, we jumped out, the police officer tried to stop him, but he drove off."

Mama J lifted her eyes towards heaven. "Jesus, Mary and Joseph."

The officer jogged to them, stopped, and crossed his arms. "I'm afraid you won't be getting your van back. He jumped the median, and the van landed on its side in some bushes with two flat tires. I'm sorry, Ladies. It's totaled. I called a tow truck and pulled the insurance card, and they'll take care of it. And here, take these bus tokens so you can get yourselves home where it's safe."

"But what about Bunny Slippers? Is he okay?" Sr. Edith said.

"A few cuts and bruises. We've hauled him to the station. He'll be fine after three hots and a cot."

"Thank you, officer."

They adjusted their habits, settled onto the curb, and pulled out rosaries.

They had only prayed through a decade before Tony arrived, good to his word. Thankfully, the phone was in one piece with only a few minor scratches. Mama J searched through her pocket for the prayer card of St. Maximillian, the saint of drug addicts and prisoners, to give him, then handed the phone to Sr. Teresa. She punched in the numbers and waited while it rang.

"Hey Irene, so, we're all okay, but, well, we had a minor incident, and we'll be a tad late. Don't worry. We'll explain when we get home."

3

MOTHER JOANNA JOINED the Sisters of Mercy when she was twenty-two. She had been a pilot in the air force when she felt the call. Oh, how she loved being in the skies, looking down at the dotted landscape, seeing God's wonders from above. And the sense of being near God in the heavens. There was nothing like it.

That's when she decided she wanted to serve Him. She hadn't flown since, but who knew if God wouldn't have a purpose in mind to use her skill. She was after all, at His service.

She stood in her simple bedroom, walls painted *Mary* blue, finished dressing, tucked her short hair under her coif and adjusted her veil.

As promised, she would take her girls to Hope House today. The war overseas had been going on for nearly two years. Parents had thought it best to send their children to safety in the U.S. And if by some unimaginable chance the parents were killed, at least there would be a generation to take their place. Why Lord? *There will be wars and rumors of wars.*

Mother Joanna walked down the hall, her sensible black shoes making a small padding sound on the wood floor. The doorbell rang, and she answered to find a man holding a large paper grocery bag. At first glance, she thought it might be a food donation. Then she read his shirt—*Your Life's a Wreck, We're Here to Help.*

"Ma'am, here are items that were left in your van. We thought you might like to have them back."

She looked from the bag to his eyes. "We would indeed. Thank you. That was very thoughtful."

He touched his ball cap and left. She nearly backed over Sister Agnes who was peering over her shoulder.

"What is it? Do you want me to take it for you?"

Mama J nodded. "We don't have time to fool with it now. We'll be late to Hope House, and we don't want to disappoint the kids. You know how excited they get when we come. It's all Brother Ben can do to keep them from running out the front door to us."

The nuns lifted their tunics so as not to trip on the steps as they departed the city bus. The children were three deep at the window, their excited faces waiting, their squeals sifting through the thin panes of the large picture window. Sr. Teresa pulled open the squeaky iron gate, and they walked the cobblestone path to the open wooden door, carrying boxes of clothing with some sweets hidden at the bottom.

"Settle down, children. Our friends will be here all day. You'll each get a chance to enjoy them." Brother Ben's deep voice was calming. He was a large man, broad shoulders, full beard, twinkly eyes and had a love for these children like no other.

"Come. Come in." He patted Mother Joanna's shoulder. "We were just getting ready for lunch."

Sr. Ignacia leaned her tall dark body down and took the hands of Vova and Bohdan and led them to the stack of plates at the end of the table, counting them and asking them how many they should each take to have an even amount. They set the table along with Mykita and Olena who put out silverware while Liliya and Bohdan placed glasses at each spot.

"What did you bring us?" The top of Mykyta's brown head came up to Irene's hip. Her whole body shook with excitement. Irene tussled her hair.

"Some clothes. New shoes. And a surprise."

"A surprise? Olena—they brought a surprise!"

Olena's deep eyes grew wide.

Brother Ben brought out a cart loaded with peanut butter and jelly sandwiches, sliced apples, and milk. Ivan reached for a sandwich as the sisters helped distribute them.

"Ivan, you have to wait!" Olena grabbed his wrist. Ivan's head sunk and his brow wrinkled.

"Hold on there, Buddy. We want to invite Jesus to bless our food first. Jesus always comes first." Sr. Ignacia began to pray.

"Bless us O Lord and these thy gifts which we are about to receive through thy bounty, through Christ our Lord."

A chorus of amens sounded. The sisters crossed themselves and squeezed onto the benches between the children throughout the long tables.

"What is your favorite thing to do here?" Irene handed the plate of sandwiches to the little blonde headed boy beside her.

"I like Brother Ben. He's so funny," Vova's tiny three-year-old voice answered.

"What does he do that's funny?"

"Sometimes he does magic!" Vova's eyes grew large. "He found a coin behind Ivan's ear."

"Yeah," Ivan said. "He even gave it to me so I could buy something."

"And one time we had boiled eggs, and he pulled one out of a scarf." Bohdan talked around a big mouthful of peanut butter.

"And sometimes he plays hide-and-seek with us." Vova

looked at Bohdan. "He always lets us win, though." Vova's eyes lit up and his shoulders raised and fell.

"That does sound like fun. When you're through eating, we'll play games. I brought dominoes and cribbage for the older ones." Irene liked anything she could construe as having a mathematical edge.

Mother Joanna drifted to Brother Ben, who stood by the wall.

"How are they adjusting? The kids?"

"I'm worried about some of them. Especially that one." He pointed his chin at Ivan. "He's always stirring up trouble. He was caught starting a fire in the garbage can last week."

"That's no good. Does he just need a friend?"

"Maybe. We're keeping an eye on him."

"And the others?"

"Surprisingly, the younger ones are doing better than the older kids. In the sibling sets, the older ones are protective of their younger brother or sister. But we've had some fights break out among them. They are so desperate to survive that they become territorial. They guard what they have and worry that someone will snatch them away again. I'm working on making them feel safe and secure."

"And teaching them, I'm sure, that their heavenly Father will always be with them and protect them. We will pray to San Jerome Emiliani."

Brother Ben nodded. "The patron saint of orphans. Even though they're not technically that. But I'm sure God knows our heart and what they need most."

WHEN THEY RETURNED to the convent, Mama J climbed the ten steps, head bent, watching for cracks in the cement. She didn't need to trip again. Last time, that mistake landed her in the ER with a sprained ankle.

When she nearly reached the top, she saw black boots and her eyes travelled past camouflaged pants and landed on a stern face. The man had to be close to seven feet tall, broad shoulders, wearing a skull cap, leather jacket and chains. He stood with his back to the wall, arms crossed, and feet spread. A second man turned from looking through the front window.

"Good afternoon, Ladies. Name's Joey. Joey Lagratto. And this here is Smols."

"Well, Joey, nice to meet you and your friend. To what do we owe the honor?"

Mama J always thought it a good idea to approach things in a congenial way. Especially when the guests were covered in tattoos and questionable attire. She wasn't trying to judge, but...

"It seems you have something that belongs to us." Joey's mouth was full of gold teeth that glinted in the sunshine as he talked.

"Really?" By this time, the rest of the sisters were gathered around Mama J. She pulled a hanky out of her pocket, dabbed it to her mouth and reached towards Joey's cheek.

"Here, let me wipe those lines off your face for you."

He shied back, shook his head and waved her hand away. She wasn't sure why he didn't want her help. She was just acting like any mom would.

"Well, would you like to come in? We have a fresh batch of cookies."

Smols sent Joey a pleading look. Mama J unlocked the door, and the men followed her in. They stood looking at the floor to ceiling bookcases, then to the spiral stairs and to the walls lined with pictures of saints. Sister Agnes turned on the fan and opened some windows while Sister Edith set a plate of snickerdoodles on the long dining room table. Mama J motioned for them to sit. Edith returned with glasses and a pitcher of milk.

"Now, tell me what you need?" Mama J closed her left hand around her right fist and met Joey's eyes, unblinking.

"It seems our friend Bernardo took a joy ride in your van." Joey reached for a cookie.

"We want to apologize for that," Smols said. His voice was deep and growly. He chomped on the cookie and closed his eyes in delight.

"It seems he left an item in the van. We just thought you might have it." Joey leaned back on the chair, leaving the back two legs on the floor.

Mama J searched the faces of each of the sisters. "Sister Agnes, I handed the bag they brought me to you, didn't I?"

"Yes, Mother. I emptied it—there was Sr. Irene's deck of cards, Sr. Edith's wrench and screwdriver, Sister Ignacia's book. Just stuff like that. I returned their items to them." She shrugged.

Joey chugged down his glass of milk and locked eyes with each nun, one by one. Edith squirmed.

"You don't seem like the kind of ladies that would lie to us now, would you?" Joey narrowed his eyes. Sr. Agnes pulled herself in.

"No sir, of course not," Mama J said. "Gentlemen, can you be more specific? What exactly are you looking for?"

Joey side eyed Smols.

4

———————

JOEY TOSSED the ping-pong ball into the air and served it over the net. Squirt rebounded. His straggly hair was held back by a teal bandana. Joey lobbed it where it bounced past Squirt onto the floor. G-Man stepped in with his paddle, and the play went on for several passes, fast and furious, matching the rhythm of the high-energy music streaming on the device. Slingshot moved in, twirling his paddle in the air several times before he hit the ball on a rebound, where it landed on the floor in front of Joey. Joey tossed his paddle onto the table and landed himself on the threadbare couch.

The dirty windows were covered by equally filthy curtains, which at one time had been navy blue. The rods could have held them straight had they not been previously used at one time as swords by Squirt and Slingshot.

Joey lifted his light gray fedora, something he was never seen without, and ran his fingers through his short hair before returning it to his head.

"I've been doing a lot of thinking."

The others gathered around. Bernardo turned his chair backwards and sat on it, his ball cap sitting backwards on his head. Squirt held a paddle and repeatedly tossed the ball up and down, the pop, pop, pop enough to make him want to pull out his hair. Joey gave him the *look,* and he quit.

"You guys remember when we were in the clink?" Slingshot's scarecrow body shuddered.

"Remember, I pointed out Big Red? He was the leader of the gang I was in. That son of a biscuit killed my little bro. And he's due to be released at the end of the month."

They all nodded. Slingshot's straight blonde bangs hung down to his eyes under his backwards ball cap. Both looked as if they hadn't been washed since The Godfather was filmed.

"We need to stick him, and that means we only have a few weeks to clean out his goods while his goons are without a leader."

"What's the take?" G-man squinted his eyes and crossed his tattooed arms—skulls and snakes with sharp fangs.

"He got away with thirty million by my estimate. And I want to take it all. It's time for him to feel some pain." Joey's long-haired chihuahua Rosie jumped into his lap. He cupped her face and rubbed noses. Her wet tongue licked his face, her big black eyes expectant.

"Thirty million? You sure about that?" Slingshot's eyebrows knit together.

"Of course, I'm sure. So, here's the plan." Joey brought a map onto the large screen TV. "G-man, you're on surveillance. I want a record of everyone's patterns of actions every day. Every moment."

G-man nodded.

"Let's give it a couple of days and see what you comes up with."

MAMA J WALKED the cobblestone path from the small chapel behind the convent from morning mass, replaying the message of creating peace when being confronted. It was uncanny how God always provided a message that coincided with daily life. She thought they had managed Joey and Smols well. Because really, what defuses tension faster than cookies and milk?

Mama J couldn't believe her eyes when she looked out the front window to the curb. Fr. David jumped out of a shiny new slate gray, twelve-passenger van. He took the steps two at a time. She opened the door before he had time to knock.

"Mother Joanna."

"Father David—you've got a new van."

"Yep, as always, God is our provider. When the parish heard what "A brand stinkin' new van? And the last one was on its last legs. Er, wheels." Her smile reached from ear to ear. "We were just getting ready to take the bus to the park where we plan to meet the children."

He handed her the keys attached to a keychain with St. Christopher, the saint of safe travels.

"Yes, I'll see you there shortly. Enjoy your new ride."

The sisters were giddy with excitement when they loaded up, running their hands over the soft upholstered seats. And since they were having a normal cold November day, when Mama J turned on the heater, they thought they had died and gone to heaven.

Brother Ben and the kids were kicking the soccer ball across the soft grassy field when they arrived. He had set up portable end goals and cones to mark the boundaries of the field. Cries of joy came when the kids spotted the sisters. From a distance, the sisters resembled blue jays with their sensible black shoes and green and purple habits.

"Hey, they're here. Come on." Mykita motioned for the others to follow. Vova squealed as his little three-year-old legs barreled into the sisters, where they were met with open arms and hugs.

"Well, I guess it's time to take a short break. Run on over to the water cooler and get drinks. Then we'll divide our guests between your teams." He set the soccer ball on the ground beside him.

"Look at what we drove up in." Mama J pointed. "Fr. David brought it to us today."

"Wowza. That's really nice."

"Right?" Mama J chugged down a cup of water and told him what happened. She scanned the field.

"Okay, girls, gather your teams."

They helped the kids take their places. Brother Ben blew the whistle, and the play began. Vova kicked the ball and landed on his rear. He quickly jumped up and chased after the ball. Taras, on a middle school growth spurt, was on the opposing team, blocked the ball and sent it in the opposite direction. Mykita ran towards it and returned it, her braids trailing behind her as she kicked it high into the air. It went out of bounds and rolled into the woods.

"I'll get it." Ivan chased after the ball, which had landed behind the hedge. Taras had a hand on his hip, getting antsy waiting for him to return.

It was taking too long. Mama J jogged to where she had last seen the ball headed. There he was, talking to a guy who looked vaguely familiar. She stopped at the edge of the hedge.

"Hey kid, nice ball." It was Tony, the man who had returned their cell phone. He kicked the ball up and down using fancy footwork.

"Give it to me." Ivan reached for it. Tony grabbed it and held it over his head. He laughed.

"Give it to me!"

"You want the ball, kid?" Tony glanced my way. "Here. I was

just messin' with ya'." He tussled Ivan's hair, then bent and whispered in his ear. He handed him a small piece of paper, which Ivan stuck in his pocket.

Ivan nodded and grabbed the ball.

"Here's a piece of gum. That always helps make you a better player." Ivan took it, and a grin stretched across his lips. This was a treat he seldom had and reminded him of his dad, who always gave him gum. Would Ivan ever see him again? He ran back to the group.

Mama J stepped up. "Tony, how nice to see you again."

Tony glanced around. "Yeah, I was just passing by."

"Well, take care of yourself. We've been praying for you." She smiled.

"Uh, yeah. Thanks." He put his hands in his pockets and shifted his eyes.

What was there about Tony? First, he returns their cell phone after telling them he would have sold it for drugs. Now he's messing with Ivan. Was he just playful? Or was there something more? And why did he give him that slip of paper? Lord, keep an eye on him and grant him grace.

⸻

DARK THUNDERCLOUDS COVERED THE SKY, threatening rain. The soccer game had ended, and Mama J and Brother Ben had taken the kids for ice cream, a rare treat. They jumped as a loud clap of thunder exploded and buckets of rain poured down.

"I just love a good storm." Sr. Agnes clapped her hands. Mama J loved a good storm too, now that they had windshield wipers that actually cleared the water from the window.

When they returned to the convent, Mama J took the front door key in her hand and made her way up the steps. What she saw when she opened the door stopped her in her tracks. A lamp lay on its side, books had been thrown off the bookshelves, and the coffee table was smashed. She turned to the right, where kitchen stools were upended, broken plates littered the floor.

Her jaw dropped as she moved aside to let the others in. They just stood there, mouths agape. What in heaven's name happened? Each sister headed to her room, stepping carefully over broken lamps and splintered chairs. The entire house had been ransacked. Drawers were pulled out, and clothing scattered everywhere. Even bathroom cabinets had been scooped out.

"Come on down, sisters. Find a place to sit. Everyone take a deep breath."

"Who would do this?" Sr. Teresa put her arm around Sr. Edith, whose cheeks were wet with tears.

"Is this what happens when we give ourselves to God?" Sr. Agnes asked. She frowned and clenched her fists.

"We need to ask what He wants us to learn. Compassion? Forgiveness?" Sr. Ignacia's eyes travelled to the crucifix above the door.

"I don't know. But it's part of God's plan. We may not grasp it now, but let's wait and see. He'll use it for good." That's when Mama J's eyes fell on a note tacked to the wall with a knife blade.

5

THE ROAR of the vacuum and the citrus smell of cleaning sprays filled the convent. Ignacia, with braided black hair covered with a bandeau, took charge, pairing Agnes with Teresa in the kitchen. She directed Irene in the common room and Edith with Mama J in charge of bathrooms and bedrooms. Times like these gave Mama J holy goosebumps—made her feel like she was leading them the way God intended. It didn't hurt to have the girls resemble Martha now and then. They spent enough time each day being Mary, sitting at the feet of Jesus. Ignacia started humming a song about being humble servants, which the others joined.

Sister Edith followed Mama J upstairs to the bathroom, carrying a broom and rags. They passed the three bedrooms, which each housed two nuns.

"I guess we should pick up what isn't broken, then sweep. What a mess!" Mama J pulled on some gloves.

"It was probably Joey and his friends that messed it all up," Edith said.

"Whatever they're looking for must be very important. I

wonder what they want it for." Mama J picked up the toilet paper rolls and set them back on the shelf.

"Maybe you don't really want to know. I mean, he smells like he could be trouble." Edith started sweeping the floor, lotion oozing between broken glass, toothbrushes under washcloths, and Q-tips strewn in a crosshatch pattern.

"I agree. But God has sent him here for a reason. We have to look past this mess and ask Him to give us eyes to see as He does."

Edith stopped and stared at her. She shook her head. "I guess I have a lot to learn."

Ignacia leaned against the door. "Mother, Brother Ben is here with a few of the kids to help clean."

Mama J pulled her head out of the plastic garbage bag where she had just dumped another dustpan of glass. "Wonderful." She wiped the sweat from her brow with a hanky from her pocket.

The stomp of boys' feet on the wooden stairs made her smile.

"I want to help Sister Edith," Ivan said.

"Well, we're almost finished here, and then you can help clean her room."

Edith smiled and put her hand on Ivan's head, his brown hair soft under her fingers.

"Thank you, Ivan. I'd love your help."

He grinned. Brother Ben cinched the top and hoisted the black garbage bag as he left.

Mama J walked next door to Edith's room, where she glanced around at the carnage—in complete contrast to house rules that the sisters make their beds daily and keep items off the floor, and clothes in their drawers. In this case, it wasn't their fault. Fortunately, nothing in this bedroom was broken. But two things caught her eye. A bottle of red fingernail polish. And a cellphone. Mama J would need to have a conversation with Edith later.

She left Edith and Ivan and went downstairs to check on the others. The place was beginning to sparkle like a new. She guessed this was one way to force the girls to deep clean. God does have a sense of humor.

With the kitchen now in order, Mama J helped with lunch. The garbage was filled with broken dishes, so Mama J laid paper towels on the table for plates and began making bologna sandwiches. Liliya sidled up to her, wrapping her arms the size of pipe cleaners around her waist.

"Would you like to help? You can lay this loaf of bread out on the counter. We'll make an assembly line."

"Olena, come help us." Liliya raised her arm and motioned her over.

"I'll spread the mayo, Olena can distribute the bologna and Liliya can add lettuce and close it up."

"I used to help my mom do this. We made lunch for my dad every day." Olena's eyes focused on her hands.

"I bet you miss them terribly."

"Yeah. I do." Her lower lip trembled.

"It was horrible," Liliya added lettuce. "We had to go underground to the bomb shelter every day. The roar of the planes and bombs squealed. I hated that."

"It was so scary," Olena said. "I hope my parents are safe." Moisture glittered on the tips of her eyelashes.

Mama J couldn't imagine what they had been through. They were too young to have suffered the tragedies they had seen. Sometimes life was so overwhelming.

She left them to set the sandwiches out while she returned upstairs to let Edith and Ivan know lunch was ready. As she reached the top of the stairs, she heard Ivan squeal.

"I found it! This is it!"

Edith was confused. "What is it? It's just a Rubik's Cube."

"I know. But this is it." He started twisting the squares. Ivan dug in his pocket and showed them a piece of paper, folded into a tiny square. When he opened it, there were two words. Rubik's Cube.

"I have to give it to Tony. He said he'd give me my own soccer ball if I did."

Edith locked eyes with Mama J, who put a hand on Ivan's shoulder.

"Ivan, may I keep it safe for you? Run down and get some lunch. I'll make sure Tony gets it."

Ivan reluctantly gave it to her.

"Don't worry. I'll give it to him so you can get your soccer ball."

Edith picked up the cube and began twisting it.

"Edith, take off your shoes and socks." She looked like Mama J had caught her sneaking out a window.

She reluctantly kicked her sensible black shoes off, sat and slowly peeled off her socks, the ones that should have been black, but instead were blue with yellow cats on them. Edith could be a little sassy at times and liked to push the envelope. Bright red toenails wiggled themselves free.

Mama J put her hands on her hips and willed Edith's eyes to meet hers. A vee creased her forehead. She nervously twisted and turned the Rubik's Cube.

"I know, I know. But it's just so hard." Edith matched yellow rows with a white center remaining.

"What's so hard?"

"Having to be the same as everyone else. I feel like I've lost my identity." She twisted a row of reds into place, leaving a yellow center.

Mama J sat down on the bed next to her. "You haven't though. Identity isn't in what you wear or what you have. It's in your character. In what you believe. In your integrity. Don't you think that God made you unique? No one in the world is like you. No one has your thoughts, your creativity, your spirit. Dressing like your sisters doesn't remove you from yourself."

"Are you going to make me do something for being bad?" Edith now had the blues, yellows, and reds in rows. She set the cube down.

"I'm going to ask you to do something, yes, but your actions are separate from you. I want you to write a list of who God sees you as. Dig into your Bible and see what you can find."

Edith handed her socks to Mama J and dutifully pulled her black pair out of her drawer and slowly slid one over her heal, like this was the last act to accepting her future life. She picked up the cube once more and made a last turn so that all sides were solid green except one red in the center. She held her thumb on the red and jolted as it fell into two pieces. Inside held a tiny thumb drive. Her mouth dropped open, and she held it up.

"Are you thinking what I'm thinking?" Mama J took it from her and placed it in her pocket.

"Joey?"

Edith nodded, not sure what her next move would be. Edith slipped the cube pieces back together, turning it so that all sides were mixed up.

"Come downstairs as soon as you're ready. We're going on a Rosary walk around the neighborhood. Perhaps God will tell me what I should do."

THE AIR WAS CRISP. Orange and red leaves drifted to the lawns and sidewalks. Fall was Mama J's favorite time of the year. She was tired of the heat, and autumn brought hope. It also made her hot habit bearable.

She and the sisters walked down the sidewalk, and at the end of each decade paused at whichever house they were in front of. They took a moment of silent prayer for the inhabitants. Prayers for health, blessings and provision.

They had nearly gone around the block when they stopped at the last house, a brownstone. It could use a good pressure washing. The windows hadn't been cleaned in years—it was a wonder anyone could see out of them. Cigarette butts, tossed and stomped, lay on the steps.

The nuns stood, rosaries in hand, and prayed. Mama J touched her throat where a lump formed, and tears stung her eyes. *Heavenly Father, bless those in this house. They seem like lost causes. Guide their choices. Use them for your glory. St. Jude, patron saint of hopeless causes and desperate situations, hold them in your hands.*

She wasn't sure who lived there or what was going on. But God knew. And now he had laid them on her heart.

6

SISTER IGNACIA THREW on an apron and bustled around the kitchen, flitting from one thing to another like a hummingbird. Her long, tiny, black braids were pulled back and held together with a rubber band. She had her favorite Kenyan food recipe memorized from when she had been a girl in Nairobi where her Bibi had made homemade chapati every day and laced each dish with fresh avocados from their giant tree. She laid out the ingredients for githeri, the bean and corn stew, on the counter. Come to think of it, she hadn't heard from her Bibi in awhile. She wondered how she was doing.

"Agnes, could you take these onions and start browning them? I'll get the flour and oil ready to pat out the chapati bread."

Agnes heated up the skillet. She peeled onions and chopped them, stopping now and then to wipe tears with the corner of her apron. They sizzled as she tossed them into the hot oil.

"Mmm, that smells so good. I need to get the coconut milk." Agnes made her way to the pantry, searching the shelves, which wasn't difficult as they were getting low on supplies. She removed three cans from the wire shelves, then stopped. Behind the shelf was a small wooden door handle. Funny she hadn't noticed that before.

"Ignacia, come take a look at this." Ignacia set a pan of water for the beans on the stove and moved to the pantry. "Help me move this shelf—it looks like there's a door. I wonder where it goes."

"You know these old houses. There were always hidden places. I think because they hid slaves."

"You don't think there would be slaves down there now, do you?" An uneasy feeling gripped Agnes.

"Ignacia, that was hundreds of years ago." Agnes shook her head.

Ignacia took the lead. "Ready?" She slid the door on creaky hinges which led to a set of wooden steps down to a dark basement. She felt around for a light switch but found none. Sister Agnes pulled a cell phone from her pocket and tapped the flashlight.

"You have a cell phone? Where'd you get that?"

"Ummmm," Sister Agnes shifted her eyes. "You have to admit it comes in handy."

"Does Mama J know?" Ignacia put her hand on her hip and shook her head.

The heavy door creaked as they shoved it open. They took slow steps down the worn uneven steps into the musty space. How long had it been since anyone had been there?

"What do you think is down here besides cobwebs, Agnes? It's kind of spooky."

"Probably just some old junk—old boxes, jars, who knows."

They jumped as a bat flew by. "Maybe we should go back." Agnes' voice trembled and she grabbed onto the back of Ignacia's veil.

"You're a chicken. Let's at least get to the bottom and look around." Agnes shone the light side to side as they took the bottom step. A large room lay in front of them, the air heavy and musty. Wooden shelves lined the walls with dusty canning jars filled with pickles, maybe apple-sauce—it was hard to tell. They were covered with dust. Lots of dust.

On one wall were stacks of boxes. Who knew what they held. Agnes squealed when a rat snuck out from behind a box and ran towards them. It's beady little eyes held theirs and then it turned and ran under the stairs.

"I've had enough." Agnes turned, but Ignacia grabbed her shoulders.

"You can't go." Ignacia pointed her towards the middle of the room. It was empty but for one thing.

A man lay motionless. Agnes sucked in a quick breath and let out a yelp, which echoed off the walls. They cautiously took one slow step after another where a puddle of thick blood oozed from his chest onto the cement.

Agnes whispered, "Do you think he's alive?"

"I'm not sure. Let me find out." Ignacia looked at his vacant, staring eyes. She gave an involuntary shudder. Who was this man? Agnes' cellphone light gave off an eerie glow, casting heavy shadows from the man.

He wore a clean ball cap with a sports team logo and was clean-shaven. Ignacia found his wrist under the rolled-up sleeves of what had been a white button-down shirt. Squatting down, she was surprised when she felt his wrist for a pulse and he moved. Was that an involuntary movement? She looked at Agnes, eyes wide.

"Lord have mercy! What happened?" Agnes' hand went to her mouth.

What happened? It didn't take a rocket scientist to tell. "He's been shot in the chest. But Agnes, I think he's still alive!"

Ignacia's eyes travelled from his hand to his face. His eyes blinked, causing his eyebrow ring to move. Slowly. Then again. She heard a faint sound and saw his lips part.

"Have to...."

Ignacia frowned. "Have to? Have to what?"

"Have to get...." He closed his eyes again.

She leaned closer to him.

"...the cube." Blood gurgled from his mouth, and he breathed his last.

"Oh no. Oh no. Oh no." Agnes put her hand to her mouth. "We better tell Mother."

They ran up the steps where they heard the alarm screeching as smoke filled the kitchen.

―――――

IT DIDN'T TAKE LONG for the police to arrive. Officer Bradley and several others, all wearing headlamps, stomped down the stairs to the dark basement. There was no sense taping off the stairs, as that seemed to be the only entry point. Ignacia and Agnes stood staring at the top of the stairs.

Officer Bradley barked orders. "Sammy Jerard, mark off where the victim is lying." Sammy pulled out a large piece of chalk and drew around the body. "He was shot through the chest with a single shot. What angle would you say?"

"It appears to have been point blank. So, whoever shot him was right here with him," Tim Hansen said and snapped multiple photos as he circled the man.

Sammy's blonde hair fell over her shoulder as she crouched and shone her light slowly around where he lay.

"I don't see any footprints."

She checked the soles of his black combat boots. They had signs of dirt.

"There must be some clues on them to show us where he's

been. I need someone from forensics to remove his boots and take them to the lab. Tim?"

Tim nodded at Sammy and pulled out a large clear bag, into which he placed the boots.

Officer Bradley crouched, observing the blood pattern.

"That nun was correct. He just died today. The blood is fresh." His eyes swept the room. "How in the heck did he get in here? It had to be something other than the stairs. He'd have to move the pantry shelves, and the nuns would have known. And he'd have booked it out of there after he shot this guy."

Sammy made a slow sweep around the room. No windows. Shelves of canned goods. A few boxes. There was no sign of their being moved. She might have to return to give a closer examination.

Lights flashed as more photos were taken, illuminating the old stone walls. They laid Mr. Deadman on a stretcher, covered him with a white sheet, and took him to the mortuary's waiting minivan.

A short, husky officer walked up to Mama J.

"Mother, I'm sorry about this poor guy. Do you have any idea how he got down there?"

"Officer, I have no idea. I didn't even know there was a basement before today." Mama J picked up a towel and waved the remaining smoke out of the window and moved the scorched cast-iron skillet to the sink.

"Did you or the others hear any shots?"

Mama J turned to the girls crowded around her, her eyebrows raised. They each shook their heads.

Officer Bradley turned to Sammy. "Must have been a silencer on the gun." Then he turned back to Mama J. "Has there been anything else suspicious?"

Did he mean other than the vandalism? Or Joey coming by? She reached into her pocket and fingered the thumb drive. She should probably give it to him. But for some reason, she felt reluctant to do that. And then there's the matter of Mr. Deadman's last words. What in heaven's name did God have in mind?

―――――

BERNARDO WAS CONSUMED with finding a job.

He'd looked everywhere, but unfortunately, it seemed people didn't want to hire guys with a felony. What was the sense of getting out? At least in jail, he didn't need money to survive. No, he had to do something. Joey hadn't given him a timeline for when he'd get paid, not to mention that he was none too happy that he botched the whole Rubik's Cube deal. How was he to know that the cube he grabbed when he wrecked the van wasn't the same one?

Bernardo was sure he wouldn't have a pocket full of money until after the big heist against Big Red. Amelia's meds were going to be in the thousands, and he had to find a way to pay for them. He had missed out on two years of her life. He wasn't about to miss out on anymore.

7

BERNARDO HOPPED out of a white panel van and confidently walked up the steps to the front door of an estate. He set his toolbox on the porch and rang the doorbell, then took a deep breath. While he waited, he took in the full front porch. In the yard, a teak bench hung from a chain connected to a great maple and moved rhythmically. The tree towered over the porch roof, colorful reds and oranges drifting down onto the green lawn. A squirrel skittered up the trunk. He wished he had grown up in this idyllic house instead of the piece of trash he had grown up in. Maybe life would have taken a much better path.

"Yes?" A middle-aged man with a shaved head and long beard greeted him.

"You called an electrician?"

The man looked at the logo on Bernardo's blue shirt.

"Yes, come in. I've got an outlet in the bedroom that shot sparks the other day. I'd like you to check it out. I don't want my house burning down." A nervous laugh.

"I'd be happy to take a look." Bernardo took in the spiral staircase, the sparkling glass chandelier hanging from a long gold chain casting rainbows on the white walls. A stone fireplace graced the open-concept great room, with round logs stacked in a loop log holder ready to cozy up to on a cold day.

A perfect setting for a huge party. Think of the card games and ping-pong table they could set up here. Bunny Slippers felt the rush of breaking in and looking for loot, that familiar tingle up his arms, a quickened heart rate, and an all-round thrill.

"Follow me up, and I'll show you what I'm talking about."

The carpet was like a blue river winding down the staircase. Bernardo had no doubt he could find either a cache of jewelry or loads of dough. *Amelia baby, don't you worry. Daddy's gonna fix things for you.*

"Look here at this outlet." It was blackened, and the center was melted.

"Yep, looks like a short. I'll need to shut off your breaker first. Will being without electricity be a problem?"

"Yes, of course. The breaker's in the closet at the end of the hall. Will you be okay if I leave you here? I've got some phone calls to make."

"Yep. No problem." *No problem at all. Just what I was hoping for.* He made a quick sweep of the bedrooms, looking behind picture frames, in closets, and under beds. He found a jewelry box with pearls, a diamond necklace, and a ruby ring. He pilfered them, shoveling them in his pocket, being careful to close the lid and leave the box as he found it. Then he returned to the den where the faulty wire was.

A large rolltop desk sat on one wall, with file folders neatly stacked and tidy envelopes in cubbies. His eyes lingered on a pencil can decorated with a child's painted handprint. He moved a grey upholstered ottoman from the wall, looking for another outlet that might have evidence of sparks. His eyes widened at the wall safe. Bernardo had been cracking safes since he was fifteen. This was going to be child's play.

"Hi."

Bernardo jerked his head around to see a young girl in a wheelchair.

"Whatcha doing?"

"I'm, uh, fixing this electrical wire." He slid the ottoman back into place and opened his toolbox.

"What's wrong with it?" She moved her chair closer. Her thin legs extending from her flowered dress looked lifeless.

"I think it has a short." He pulled out his screwdriver.

"Can I do that? I know how to use tools." He paused taking her in—intense dark eyes, sparkly black hair. Reminded him of Amelia. Even looked the same age.

"Sure. Take the cover off, but then I need to do the rest. I don't want you to get hurt."

He grabbed the circuit tracer transmitter from the box and isolated the wire. Thank goodness for YouTube. He snipped the wire and stripped the ends.

"Celia, what are you doing in here?"

"Just watching, Daddy. I want to learn how to do that."

"Don't mind her—she's always curious."

"She reminds me of my daughter." Bernardo held back a grimace.

"Celia, come on down. It's time for your medicine."

Bernardo watched them leave. This wasn't going to work. How could he prey on them? This was too close to home. He wrapped up the job, returned the jewelry and sat in the van with his head on the steering wheel. What was he going to do now?

His head jerked up as he heard tapping on the window. He started the van and rolled the window down. The owner of the house stood there.

"Hey, I really appreciate the work you did. I know you guys aren't paid enough. I just wanted to give you a bonus for doing such a good job and keeping us safe." He handed Bernardo an envelope.

"Wow, um. Thank you. I'm not sure what to say."

The man grinned, gave a two-finger salute, and walked back to the house.

Bernardo opened the envelope, where ten one-hundred-dollar bills had been placed, and shook his head.

SISTER IGNACIA HUMMED as she laid the lasagna noodles precisely in rows in a large aluminum pan. How did that man get into their basement? There were no windows. They hadn't seen any other doors. But then again, it had been dark, and the shelves and boxes had cast lots of shadows.

She stirred the tomato sauce, added a leveled cup of sauteed onions and two tablespoons of fresh oregano. The pot bubbled, and she breathed in the tantalizing aroma. Had he been shot in the basement? There was no sign he had been drug, and the pool of blood was under and around him. And she could tell the bullet had gone right through him, which would mean it was shot from a close range. Who knew that her training as an investigator pre-sister would lead to an opportunity such as this?

She crossed herself and prayed for the poor man's soul. "Saint Joseph, patron saint of departing souls, pray for us." She layered the sauce, noodles, and spicy ground sausage with a mixture of Parmesan and mozzarella cheeses.

She had to go down and investigate further. There was more to this story than they knew.

8

AN HOUR LATER, as the sun was starting to set, Sister Ignacia and Mama J walked to the back door of the neighbor's house, the raggedy one she had stopped in front of while on their Rosary walk the other day. She opened the ripped screen door, weathered paint peeling in curls, and rapped. A small dog yipped its protective high-pitched bark.

"Rosie, shut up!"

A large bald man peeked window. He pulled the door open, put his hand on the doorframe above his head and leaned into it.

"Well, what do we have here?"

Mama J's eyes travelled up to a man wearing a skullcap, chains hanging from his neck, and gauges in his ears. His head nearly touched the ceiling.

"Smols?" She placed her hand over her mouth. "I had no idea this was your house."

"Well, it is. What do you want?"

A smaller man stood behind Smols chugging a can of Squirt. He wore his ball cap backwards, and his white tank top showed a lack of muscles.

"The Lord told us to bring you a tray of lasagna." Mama J didn't mean for her hands to shake and tried to still them, so that she wouldn't drop the pan.

"Now ain't that something. We was just wonderin' what would be for dinner." Squirt elbowed Smols who swatted him away.

"Act like a gentleman, Squirt, if that's even possible. Ladies, would you like to come in?"

They followed them through the kitchen into the living room with Smols leading the way.

"Gentlemen, we've got company."

"I'll get some plates." Squirt chugged the last of the can and tossed it on the floor amidst a chips wrapper and an apple core.

"You'll want to eat it soon while it's still hot. We took it out of the oven twenty minutes ago at 350 degrees, so it would now be 325 degrees—the perfect temperature," Sister Ignacia said.

"Hey Joey, we got company," Squirt hollered.

Joey came down the stairs and jumped off the last two steps.

"Joey? This is your house? We didn't know." Mama J couldn't believe this was where God had sent them.

His mouth turned up in a slow grin. He waved his outstretched arm around the room. "Welcome to our digs. Have a seat."

He motioned to a faded plaid couch. This felt like going into the lion's den. Had Daniel been this nervous?

Tony set paper plates on the coffee table and took the lasagna from Sister Ignacia. He peeled off several paper towels and then dished up.

"What's that delicious smell?" Slingshot placed a bean into his slingshot and pulled the pouch back, aiming it at a tortoise, which slowly plodded across the wood floor.

Smols grabbed Slingshot's right arm as he pulled back on his device ready to shoot.

"I wouldn't think about harming my pet if I were you."

Slingshot squirmed. "I was just playin' around. You don't have to get all bossy."

Sister Ignacia and Mama J glanced at each other, crossed themselves and said the blessing.

"I remember when I was a little boy, my grandma took me to Mass." Smols held his fork to his lips. "There was this one nun who always made me feel special." He looked at the ceiling. "She's the one who taught me how to play ping-pong. Sister Monica ping ponica." He nodded towards the ping-pong table behind them with a smile the memory brought.

Mama J slid a glance at Sister Ignacia and held back a grin.

Squirt popped open another can and took a drink. "When I was little, we went to Vacation Bible School. Had all those flannel graph stories. I got to put up the figures of Jesus and the 'ciples.'"

"And sing songs—what was that one called? The one we got to show our muscles?" Smols said.

"He is weak, but we are strong." Squirt gulped down the rest and let out a loud belch.

Slingshot popped him on the head. Ignacia couldn't help but note that there was a rip in the sleeve of his blue plaid shirt. Maybe she could bring over a needle and thread and fix that for him.

"No, no, no. We are weak, but He is strong."

"Ain't nobody gonna help us out. We be strong in our own right," Joey said. He finished his plate and loaded up on seconds.

If only he knew the truth. The door squeaked shut as Tony and Squirt walked out with cigarettes and a lighter, leaving Smols and Joey with Ignacia and Mama J.

"Joey, I'm not sure what you've got going on, but we're all praying for you. Every day."

"Well, Lady, I'm not counting on that helping, but I'm sure it's not going to hurt anything. There's just one thing I need to ask. It's been nagging at me since the first time we stopped by your place."

Mama J reached over and placed her hand on Joey's knee. "Why, what is it, Joey?"

"We never found what we was looking for." Joey looked around the room. David fidgeted with his slingshot. Mama J tilted her head.

"Did you ever find a Rubik's Cube?"

Agnes shrank into the couch. In a small whisper she ventured, "Yes."

"You did?" Joey sat up straight and leaned in.

She bent her head in a barely perceptible nod.

"Could you bring it to me? Or I could follow you home and you give it to me?" Joey was beside himself. Energy pulsed through his body. Finally—this would be the final stab at his nemesis.

Mama J removed her hand from his knee. She bowed her head a moment, then looked at Joey. She reached into her pocket and extracted the item she'd been holding onto.

"That won't be necessary." She held her fist to Joey. "Take this." She dropped the weird looking thumb drive into his waiting hand.

Joey held back a smile and nonchalantly said, "Thanks." He placed it into his shirt pocket.

"I need to tell you something else." Mama J sucked her lower lip between her teeth.

He leaned back on the couch and put his hands behind his head. He was plenty relaxed. But Mama J? She clasped her hands together as her heart pounded ka-thunk, ka-thunk like a flat tire on a car.

"We found a dead body in our basement. You wouldn't happen to know anything about that, would you?"

JOEY LAY on the couch with Rosie in his lap watching a crime show. This is where he got his best ideas. Why reinvent the wheel? Just adapt what some screenwriters figured out already.

He couldn't shake the nuns finding Michael dead in their basement. It wasn't that he hadn't deserved to die. He had been the only one who wasn't caught in Big Red's heist when Joey had been part of the gang. Michael was a monster—a mere step down from the brutality of Big Red. When they had been released, Joey sought Michael out. He had to find out where Michael had buried Robbie. That is if he actually did. For all he knew, he had pitched his little bro into the river where he'd never be found. That lying son of a turnip led him down several rabbit trails with false information. Joey had had enough and directed Slingshot to take him out. He hadn't counted on his not realizing that the hidden door in the cellar led to the convent basement.

Well, it was out of his hands now.

"Right, Rosie?" He stroked her head, and she licked his hand.

The cops wouldn't have any way of knowing who killed Michael. That wasn't what he was worried about. What plagued him, for one, was that now the nuns were involved. Involving innocent people was never in his plan. Especially those that might have an in with God.

He wasn't sure he believed in the fable of a god, but what if there really was one? Those crazy women said they were praying for him. That could be a bad thing. A really bad thing. He wasn't an angel, and there was no way their god was going to want to do anything positive for him. Nope, not with the kind of lifestyle he lived and what he'd done.

For two, he had to find his baby bro. And he wasn't going to rest until he did. But wait. What if he asked the nuns to pray that Robbie could be found? It couldn't hurt anything, could it?

Joey looked back at the TV to watch a car chase ending in an explosion. It revved up his adrenaline. Wouldn't that be a great way to end Big Red? Obliterate him in a massive inferno.

9

As Mama J sorted through the Thanksgiving donations brought to them for Brother Ben's kids, she couldn't stop thinking about the things that had transpired. First, having their van stolen, then there was the whole thing with Joey and his friends tearing their house apart. And Sister Agnes finding a secret door. And then to find a dead body. A *dead* body! And of course, it couldn't just end there.

She was absolutely sure that God had told her to take lasagna to those in that house. How was she supposed to know that's where Joey lived? Why, oh, why does she daily ask God to send her to the poor and forsaken? This was not what she had in mind. Her eyes travelled to the ceiling as she shook her fist in the air. It's not like God didn't know what was going on.

Then there's the matter of the thumb drive. She didn't know what's on it, but it couldn't be good if Joey was that desperate for it. Was that going to make her an accessory to a crime? Lord, have mercy!

"Mama J, how can I help?" Sister Irene's eyes drifted over the measuring utensils.

"I've sorted everything out. Let's get a head start on the pies and rolls. Which would you rather make?"

"I'm a magician at making bread. My mom shared her magic with me. But I can ask Agnes to make the pies. She has a secret crust recipe."

"SISTER AGNES... Come into the kitchen!"

Mama J covered her ears. That girl could sound the alarm if ever there need be. I guess that comes from being the youngest of fourteen. If you wanted to be heard, you had to use your voice.

Sister Agnes rounded the corner, where Irene handed her an apron.

"All the pie fixings are together here on the counter. We'll need four pies. Pumpkin, two apples and a pecan. You know how the kids like choices."

Irene rubbed her hands together. "You won't be disappointed, Mother." She pulled out a bowl and measuring cups.

Irene measured two cups of warm water, held it to her eyes to make sure it was exact and sprinkled a level tablespoon of yeast over it. "I can't wait to see the kids again. They're so fun."

"Did you hear what Ivan said last time?" Mama J shook her head, a little worried.

"He was telling us about the new friend he had met at the park and how proud he was that he was to be trusted with an important mission." She shook her head. "That guy has such a vivid imagination."

Mama J wished it were just his imagination. She didn't like the thought of his getting mixed up with those guys. He seemed to need attention, and this wasn't the kind that was going to do him any good.

She sliced apples for the pie.

"Are we going to perform a nativity play this year? I think those kids would love that." Irene held up her floured hands.

"Tomorrow would be a good time to start planning that with them. I'm sure Brother Ben would assist."

"I could bribe him with his own pie if he resisted." Irene's lips turned into a crooked grin.

"I'm sure that won't be necessary."

G-MAN PULLED on his fleece face covering and slid his grey flat cap over his head. The sun was shining in a full blue sky. Sunglasses would be a good idea. With scissors, he cut a square out of the bottom of a pop bottle and shoved it into his coat pocket. Every detail had to be thoroughly thought through. He couldn't afford any slip-ups.

A blast of cold air met him as he opened the door. He swung one leg over his bike and pedaled down the sidewalk, parking several blocks away from his destination. Staying incognito was important. He couldn't take a chance of being recognized.

Victorian houses filled the neighborhood, their turrets standing guard, smoke curling from the chimneys. A red child's bike lay against a porch railing, next to a snow shovel. G-man adjusted his wool scarf to cover his exposed neck and zipped up his jacket. He remembered his childhood, riding bikes with his older brother William, playing kick the can in the streets. William had given him the nickname from George to G-man, making him feel special.

All was good until his dad was in an accident that reduced him to a vegetable. They went from a comfortable life to one of creditors and searching for their next meal. Running drugs with William became the solution to their poverty. And if truth be told, gave him the necessary skills he needed now.

He observed the two houses, arms crossed and leaning against the neighbor's tree. It was obvious that the one on the right wasn't Big Red's. Christmas lights already adorned the porch, and a large blowup Santa and Frosty were on the lawn. He shifted his focus to the other.

The lace curtains were pulled back where G-man could see the outline of an unlit chandelier. He needed to get into the house. Place some hidden mics and a few cameras. He made his way to the back alley and peeked through a knothole into the backyard. No sign of anyone. He pulled the string on the gate latch, which clicked, and the gate slid open. He was glad there was no snow, frost or dew that would show his footsteps. Vicious barking turned his head. A Rottweiler poked its nose, sharp teeth exposed, through a broken board and pushed against it. G-man kept walking, ignoring the snarling and growls.

He stepped over the broken board on the back steps and peered through the kitchen window where a kettle sat on the stove and canisters were on the counter. G-Man slipped the piece of plastic out of his pocket and deftly slid it through the doorjamb, sliding the knob open.

The door swung open on oiled hinges. What he saw surprised him. Unlike Joey's house, this place was pristine. At first he didn't recognize the smell of cleaning product—it was a foreign concept. No dirty dishes in the sink. Unlike theirs, a lid on the trash can kept trash from falling all over the floor. A rat wouldn't have been happy here—no crumbs on the countertops. A person could eat off the polished floor.

G-man shook his head and made his way to the living room, but not before he slid a mic under the counter.

G-man placed his feet on the Asian rug in the middle of the room—his ears tuned to any sounds. It was quiet—a good sign. A window seat under the large leaded bay windows held a knit throw and a book. He picked it up—a Hardy Boys mystery. Huh, he remembered reading that exact one.

He surveyed the floral wallpapered walls to see where to

place a camera. Fortunately, they were tiny and the same dark color as the swirly design of the paper. He placed one in the center of the paisley eye and headed up the carpeted stairs.

On the walls were painted portraits of men. He paused to examine them. He put his palm to his forehead. John Dillinger, Carl Gugasian, Adam Worth, Three-fingered Jack—all burglars. All heroes of the trade. He snapped photos of each–he'd look them up when he got home. See if he could get any clues as to how they worked.

At the top of the stairs, there were three rooms. The first was an office—a wooden desk with three flat-screen monitors. This was some serious business here. He placed a mic under the back lip of the desk and a camera on the window wall behind the desk. He wanted a clear view of the computer.

Muffled footsteps were in the hall. He slid the door shut with his foot. A man coughing. A toilet flushed. The sound of vomit. Another flush. G-man slunk through the door and down the stairs. He rounded the landing to the living room. The early December sun was setting. Headlights shone through the window. Time to bogey on out of there.

10

"HOW'S MY GIRL?" Bunny Slippers wrapped an arm around Amelia's waist. "You look mighty pretty tonight."

"I'm doing better, Daddy. Today I got to play outside for recess, and I didn't even get tired."

Bunny Slippers let out a sigh of relief. Perhaps he could redeem himself. Make it up to his wife and daughter. Show them that he had changed.

"She's really been a lot better." Marie set out silverware on the fall placemats. She allowed a faint smile to curve her lips.

Bernardo felt satisfaction fill his chest like a burst water pipe welling from his gut to his heart. This seemed like the turn-around they needed—both medically and relationally. His getting the money from Mr. Estate Man had been a blessing, allowing them to get treatment for Amelia. A miracle, really. The downside was he knew he'd need a lot more money if he were to keep his precious little princess healthy. Still, it would be nice if Joey came through.

JOEY PUNCHED the remote to his large TV, tuning into the pre-programmed visuals from the cameras and mics G-man had placed. He didn't want to miss anything. Details were important. Hiding those cameras at Big Red's had been a success. He sat forward in the faded lazy boy, his elbows on his knees and hands clasped, waiting to see into his house. The sleeves of his faded denim shirt were rolled up, showing his muscled forearms. Rosie stood on her little chihuahua hind legs, begging to be let up, her dark eyes begging to be loved, her tail wagging like the pendulum on a clock.

Big Red rolled a large chest to the center of the room and lifted the lid. Georgie, Moe, and several others surrounded him. "What do ya think of that, Boys?" Their eyes grew large.

Joey tensed at the sound of Big Red's voice, and his hands formed fists, his fingernails biting into his palms. Each feed brought flashes of memories—and none of them good. Joey had always had a certain respect for the man. But in the end, the guy was a crook with no room for thought or argument. And that hadn't gone so well for Joey.

Bars of gold gleamed, reflecting in the large wall mirror, the dark wooden scrolled frame contrasting with the 1800s green paisley-patterned wallpaper.

Smols stood behind Joey's chair, his massive arms crossed, and feet spread. "Take a look in the mirror. You can see the whole surroundings—a spiral wooden staircase, antique furniture, a fireplace."

"But no flames. Probably too lazy to bring in wood." G-man leaned in closer. "That chest wasn't there last week."

"The chandelier has fake candles. Look, there's a spider hanging by a thread." Squirt laughed and elbowed Slingshot. Squirt adjusted his black knit hat over his blond curls.

"Shhh. Listen up." Joey turned up the volume.

"Where ya gonna hide that, Boss? We can't just keep it here, can we?"

"Right here. Nobody's going to think to look for something that's in plain sight. We just cover it with a pretty little tablecloth and put a vase of fake flowers on top. Then we keep it here until we know the coast is clear."

Moe slid a glance at Georgie and shrugged his shoulders. *Who did he think was gonna come over to visit? A neighbor? Door Dash?*

Big Red closed the lid and wheeled it to the center of the carpet in front of the couch. Georgie dug an embroidered table-cloth from the hutch and shook it out before placing it on top. "Now ain't that gonna be a nice little coffee table? It looks just like my grannie's house."

The video ended, and Smols turned to Joey. "We gonna try to take it?" Smols' deep voice resonated off the cheap paneled walls.

"He's gotta pay. Nobody gets away with killing my little bro and lives to tell."

Joey hadn't wanted to take Robbie with him on that heist. Robbie was only ten and looked up to Joey like he was a hero. Joey had told him to stay with the neighbors—their mom wasn't going to be home from working at the dive bar until late, and who knew where their dad was sleeping off his drugs. The next thing he knew, Robbie had tailed him when the cops were closing in. Robbie was at the wrong place at the wrong time.

Joey raked his hands over his face. Rosie licked off the salty tears.

———

Mama J watched as Sister Ignacia corralled the kids for their first practice of the nativity. It was so important to have them act out the story of the greatest person to ever live. And Ignacia, with her boisterous, big personality, was the perfect one to lead the charge.

"Who knows where baby Jesus was born?" Ignacia studied the waving hands and peered into each child's eyes, their bottoms on the floor sitting crisscross. "Okay, everyone at once!"

"Bethlehem!"

Ignacia threw her hands in the air, making her dozens of micro- braids, which were pulled into a pony, shake and wave. "You are so smart. Ready for another question?"

They all nodded.

"This might be hard—who was Jesus' father?" Taras gave a slight shrug of his beefy shoulders and looked away. The classic *don't-call-on-me-cuz I don't know* look. Bohdan and Mykyta waved their hands in the air, yelling, "I know, I know!"

"Here's what we're going to do. Each of you talk it over with your neighbor for a minute, and when I snap my fingers three times, you'll shout it out. Ready?"

Ignacia held Mama J's eyes for a moment and shed a grin that was pure sunshine. She was definitely in her element. Mama J remembered when Ignacia had joined the convent. A large girl from Kenya. She would sit back and quietly observe everyone, speaking only when spoken to. Turns out she had been severely punished for basically being herself. Saying what was on her mind. Taking charge of situations and finding solutions. All things that Mama J found beautiful in her. It took some time and a lot of prayer for her to trust her. But seeing her now? She was free to be her goofy, wild, exhilarating self.

Mama J walked to Bother Ben and sat beside him. A large plastic bin filled with costumes was on the floor before them. They sorted them by character, white sheer angel smocks with halos made from wire and silver tinsel. Striped shepherd's tunics and cloth belts. Don't forget a few staffs. A long robe for Joseph and a long blue dress and shawl for Mother Mary. Crowns for the Wisemen and sheep and cow costumes, because you can't have a manger without the animals.

They raised their heads to a mixed chorus of "Joseph" and "God". Brother Ben smiled.

He stood. "All of you are right. Joseph was Jesus' earthly father, and God was Jesus' heavenly father. And isn't it neat that you all are brothers and sisters of Jesus? Because God is our heavenly father as well."

Ignacia clasped her hands together. "Well, now, children, it's time to assign costumes for the nativity play." She pulled a slip of paper from her pocket.

"I'll call your name and tell you who you will play, and then you can see Mama J and Brother Ben to get your costumes. Try them on so we make sure they fit."

It was nice to see how Ignacia had taught them to be calm and patient, knowing they would each get their turn. Well, mostly—you always had to keep an eye on Ivan.

"Iryna will be Mary, Bohdan is Joseph, Ivan is Gabriel, Taras and Liliya are Wisemen."

"I want to be a soldier, not a stupid angel." Ivan crossed his arms and glared.

"Sorry, Bud, there aren't any soldiers in this story. And Gabriel isn't just any angel. He's God's special angel."

"Who's going to be baby Jesus?" Olena put her hands out, palms up.

"Well," Ignacia put her finger to her lips, "since we have no real babies in our midst, I guess we'll use a doll."

Tears formed and ran down Olena's gaunt cheeks.

"Hey there, what's going on?" Ignacia squatted and wrapped Olena's slight body in her arms.

She took a hiccupping breath. She wiped her eyes with her thumb.

"My baby brother was killed. I wish we could have him be Jesus."

"Awww, now. You know what? He's luckier than that. He's *with* Jesus. He's probably playing with all the other kids in heaven, happy as can be."

Olena's eyes widened. "Really?"

Mama J looked to heaven. *This. It's what I've devoted my whole life to. Sharing the beauty of God's love and the end game.*

Sister Teresa and Edith set up the stage. Teresa found a box to use for the manger. Edith had taken butcher paper and made a stable background, which she taped to the back wall of the stage area. Teresa led the animals behind the manger, the shepherds and kings to the side and Mary and Joseph in front.

Teresa sent Mary onstage, where Gabriel was waiting. Ignacia took her Bible and began to read.

"Hail, favored one! The Lord is with you."

And the angel said to her, "Don't be afraid, Mary, for you have found favor with God. You will become pregnant and have a son, and you will name him Jesus."

Iryna said, "I will? That's crazy talk. I'm just a kid."

"It's true. But that's what's gonna happen, cuz it says so in the Bible. Jesus is going to be a great king, and you're gonna be his mom." Ivan shrugged his shoulders, and his wings flapped. "Don't you know that nothing is impossible with God?"

Iryna shook her head and frowned.

Ignacia continued. *"Joseph and Mary went to Bethlehem to be counted."*

Iryna linked her arm through Bohdan's elbow and followed him to the stable.

And Mary gave birth to her baby. And the angel, full of glory, returned and said," Don't be afraid. I bring you good news of great joy, which shall be for all the people, for today a savior has been born, which is Christ the Lord."

Teresa sent the other angels in where they chorused, "Glory to God in the highest and peace on earth."

Iryna handed the doll, wrapped in a blanket, to Ivan, crossed her arms, and said, "Did they really mean there would be peace on earth? Cuz maybe they needs to look around. We wouldn't even be here if that was the case. We'd be home with our parents."

Mama J looked at Brother Ben, whose eyelashes were moist. How do you help children understand big things like war? She wasn't sure *she* could wrap her mind around it. And she couldn't even imagine the horrible things they'd seen and the trauma they held on to. But she hoped to help them understand that God loves them and truly has a plan for them.

11

"COME ON, girls, we need to pack up all the Thanksgiving fixings and take them to Brother Ben's." Mama J wanted to bless Brother Ben and the kids with a good dinner and help them create new memories. Memories that were filled with fun and laughter. She hoped it could erase some of their trauma and pain.

The air was crisp, and most of the leaves had fallen off the red maples, American sweet gum, and ginkgoes. The reds, magentas and yellows were vibrant and a thrill to take in. And what wasn't to like about the damp, earthy smell? On a day like this, it was easy to be thankful.

They soon arrived at Hope House. The sisters bubbled with excitement about being with the kids. Agnes loved to take photos, so she was designated as the historian. She had created some amazing photo books and would certainly take some great shots today. And Lord willing, they'd have photos to show their parents if, and when they were reunited.

Everyone unloaded and carried the food. Mama J wasn't expecting the scene when she opened the front door of the house. The kids were scattered around the large living area, playing card games, making puzzles, building block towers and drawing. That, of course, was no surprise. The shocker was who was playing with them.

Mama J's eyebrows raised when Brother Ben took the pies from her hands.

"What are those guys doing here?" She kept her voice low.

Ben shrugged. "They showed up and said they wanted to do something nice—something that someone could say they were thankful for. You know, give back a little. So, I let them in."

Was Ben naïve? Surely, allowing their influence on these precious souls was not a wise choice.

Joey sat cross-legged on the floor helping Bohdan build a block tower, which was nearly as tall as the eight-year-old. "Here, use the smaller blocks to support a larger one. Set them carefully like this."

Joey demonstrated.

"Let me do it." Bohdan took the two from Joey and carefully placed them on the precarious tower before adding a larger one. He stood back and jumped with glee. The action caused the whole tower to collapse.

Bohdan put his hands to his cheeks. "Oh no! Now it's ruined." He slunk to the floor in a heap—head bowed between his legs.

"It's not ruined. It's just another opportunity to improve our building skills." Joey reached his hand to place it on Bohdan's back, then drew it back. It was like he was a natural with kids. Who knew? But what caused him to draw back? Was he uncomfortable with physical touch? Or did this cross a boundary for him?

It was nice to see that genuine smile on Joey's lips. He always seemed to have a lot on his mind, and the few times Mama J had seen him, he never really seemed to relax. Until now.

She turned to the table, where Smols sat with Taras playing

a game of chess. He was like a giant next to the middle schooler. Smols moved his knight into a position to force Taras' king. He sat back with his massive arms crossed, his face rigid. The boy studied the board, and you could actually see the wheels turning in his head. He moved a bishop to protect his king, placing Smols' king in check. He looked squarely at Smols.

The smile stretched across Smols' face. "You are quite the adversary, young man."

"I know. My name means ruler of the world. You don't have a chance." Taras' smile radiated to his ears.

Smols laughed at his blunt retort. "Where did you learn to play chess?"

"My dad taught me. We used to play every day before—" Taras turned away, wiped his nose on his sleeve and composed himself. "Where did you learn, Smols?"

"I had an uncle who taught me. I went to live with them when I was about your age."

"Why did you do that? I mean, move?" That was not a choice Taras would voluntarily take.

Smols cleared his throat. "Well," he looked at the ceiling, "the truth is that my parents were part of the mafia and had stolen some diamonds in '81. They ended up in jail, and I needed somewhere to go."

Taras frowned. "Are you a bad guy?"

Smols shifted in his seat. "Um, not mostly."

Sunlight streamed through the window onto the floor where Tony lay with his elbow on the floor and one hand propped under his cheek where he played with Ivan. Ivan picked up the plane they had constructed with Brother Ben's 3-D printer. Ivan held it as he flew it through the air making shooting sounds— the kind boys are so good at. Tony picked up another and flew in towards Ivan's. The plane in Ivan's hand crashed into Tony's.

"Take that, sucker. You're never gonna win the war. My men have you covered, so you may as well give up now." Ivan's shoulders tensed, and his face was determined.

"Hey. Hey, what's that all about?"

Ivan snapped out of his trance. "I hate them!"

"Who?"

"The Russians. They killed a bunch of my people."

His flash of anger gave Mama J pause. And Tony? He had an indiscernible expression—like he was relishing this side of Ivan. That couldn't be good. She would have to mention this to Brother Ben. Have him keep a closer eye on Ivan.

The green ping-pong table in the center of the room shook with action. Squirt teamed with Olena, and Slingshot joined Mykita at the other end of the table. They were well matched, with Slingshot just a head taller than Mykita and Squirt eye to eye with Iryna. Olena lobbed the ball over the net, where it bounced on the table within easy access to Iryna. She returned it with a powerful topspin, where Slingshot spun around and shot a backhanded block, earning them the winning point.

Squirt set his paddle on the table. "I'm thirsty. Let's get a drink so we can whoop them the next round."

"I'm glad I'm on Slingshot's team." Iryna smiled. "How did you get your name?"

Slingshot crossed his arms and looked at the floor. "I grew up in Alabama, and we used to shoot the crows in the cornfield with a slingshot. I had six brothers, and out of them all, I was the sharpshooter. So, they started calling me slingshot. My real name is David." He shrugged.

"My friends at home always called me shrimp cuz I'm shorter than everybody. I don't mind though. They're right. I guess it's just the way God made me." Mykita shrugged. "Do you think God made you good with a slingshot? I mean, he made David in the Bible good with one. He killed a giant."

"I don't know. I never thought about it. Maybe."

Bunny Slippers donned hot pads and took the turkey out of the oven. The heavenly odor of crusty skin filled the room. G-man took the hot, homemade rolls and placed them on a serving dish, relishing the sweet fragrance of fresh bread—something they never had. Ignacia cut the pies, and Edith filled a bowl with cranberry sauce.

Liliya ran in, chased by Bohdan.

"Hey, hey, hey—you guys settle down. You'll break something, knock something over, or burn yourself. Be nice to your sister." Mama J wrapped her arms around the two of them and knelt to look in their eyes.

"Here, Bohdan, stack the plates, and Liliya can set the silverware on the table. Ask Olena to help you." Liliya stuck her tongue out at Bohdan. The glint in his eye was a sure sign their chase wasn't done.

Bohdan began to stack the plates and glanced at Bunny Slippers. "Why do you have those bunny slippers on?"

Bunny Slippers took a large serving dish for the turkey and smiled. "They're really comfortable. Have you ever worn slippers?"

"I don't think so. They're cool. Do you think I could get some for Christmas?"

He rustled Bohdan's blond hair and laughed. "Maybe. We'll see what Santa says."

Mama J said, "It was nice of you guys to come be with the kids. They could use individual attention."

"We wanted to do something nice for a change." Bernardo's shoulders hitched, and he started to carve the turkey.

"Well, it's working. Feels good, doesn't it? To do something nice?"

G-man nodded and slid a glance at Bernardo.

Brother Ben asked everyone to bow as he crossed himself to pray.

G-man watched Joey cross himself and gestured, a puzzled look on his face.

Joey threw his hands up. "What? I grew up Catholic."

"In the name of the Father, the Son, and the Holy Spirit. We are grateful for sending these fine gentlemen to join us today. Help them know how much you love them. Please keep the parents of these children safe and make a way to reunite them. For the food you've so graciously provided, we ask your blessing. Let's eat! Oh, and if any of you are looking for work, I have a lead on some jobs." Brother Ben's eyes settled on each man in turn. Bernardo lifted his chin at Ben. It appeared he might be interested in honest labor.

The nuns dished up plates for everyone, making sure the kids held them with both hands as they walked carefully to their seats.

Joey was at the end of the line. "Mama Joanna, could I ask you something?"

"Of course, what's on your mind?

"So, I had a little brother who got shot in the middle of a heist." He looked at the floor and shuffled his feet. "We all got sent to jail for a couple years, and I never heard what happened to his body."

She paled. "That's awful. You must be devastated."

Joey cleared his throat. "I was wondering. If what Brother Ben said is really true, you know, about God loving us, maybe he could help me figure out what happened to Robbie. I don't really know how prayer works, but do you think you could ask the big guy in the sky where I could find him?"

12

MAMA J POKED her head out of her office. "Ignacia, could you come see me in my office?"

"Yes, of course."

Mama J motioned to the loveseat, where sunlight shone through the lace curtains and cast an intricate shadow on the seat. Mama J moved to join Ignacia and angled her body towards her.

"Wasn't Thanksgiving great?"

"Yes—I was so surprised to see our neighbors there. But they seemed to have a great time with the kids."

"They did. I feel terrible for not having thought to invite them myself."

"Awww Mama J, God took care of it, didn't he?"

She patted her knee. "What I wanted to talk to you about was something that happened yesterday. You know which one Joey is, right?"

She nodded. "The one with all the tattoos on his neck and head?"

Mama J nodded. "He asked me whether I would pray about a situation. Of course, I said yes. And then I thought of you."

"Really? How can I help?"

"You said you used to be an investigator before you joined Sisters of Mercy, right?"

"I did. I had spent eight years in the field."

"Here's the situation. Apparently, Joey had been in a shootout during a heist. His little ten-year-old brother Robbie had followed him."

"That's awful. A little kid?" Irene frowned and cupped her face with her fingertips.

"Joey said Robbie got shot. He believes he was killed, but the cops came on the scene and hauled them all to jail. He wants to know where Robbie's buried so he can see his grave."

Ignacia curved her index finger over her lips and supported her chin with her thumb.

"So, you want me to try to find out where he is?"

"Yes. Take it to prayer and see where God leads you."

IGNACIA CLIMBED the marble steps where her eyes travelled to the four sculpted columns, and up to *Police Department* chiseled into the stone. It was an imposing structure, to be sure. And inside held the fate of lives propelled by justice.

She set her wallet and keys in the small tray and sent it through the scanner when she entered. This was the first time she had set foot in the department wearing her habit. Her heart beat a little faster, and she took a deep breath. Would she still be shown the respect she had gained when she was employed there?

Everyone had been shocked when she announced her resignation to join the convent. They knew her as a tall, tough, no-nonsense Kenyan, a persona she had put on when she was in high school, thrust into a move to a new neighborhood after her parents' divorce. She had been bullied by a group of girls, their goth dress in sharp contrast to her designer clothes. Apparently, clothes made the woman, and assumptions about her were made without her having the chance to show who she really was. It made more sense to become assertive than to let them catfight her, or to pummel her with words meant to diminish who she was.

And now, if clothes made the woman, she embraced wearing a habit. The woman she was now was different in some respects. It seemed God had re-channeled her no-nonsense, get'er done into positive change, but he had smoothed out the rough and tough gal she had been. Of course, knowing who God thought she was had been a game changer. She had shed many tears knowing He saw her as beautiful, loved, and forgiven.

She boarded the elevator, pushed six, and regarded the others. A trim, grey-haired man cleared his throat several times and nervously fingered the middle button on his blue suit. *Lord, I don't know what conundrum this man is facing but surround him with peace and guide his steps.*

A head of curly black hair held back with a colorful bandeau held Irene's attention, reminding her of her former self. This girl could be her twin—same height, dark eyes, confident stance.

A ding alerted her to her floor. She stepped into the hall and searched the names on the doors—names she recognized. In a small way, it felt good to be back in this place that had been home for eight years, each case propelled by the search for a conclusion to someone's story.

She put her hand on the brass doorknob and entered the office of Sammy Jerard. The short blond stood from her desk and greeted her.

"Ignacia." Sammy held out her hand and embraced Ignacia's firm grip. "Thanks for meeting with me."

"Yes, of course. Have a seat. You've been missed around here. I hope your new life is treating you well."

Ignacia nodded. If truth be told, she *was* living her best life. She looked at Sammy's desk before her, covered with scattered files and paperwork. A whiteboard on the wall was covered with dozens of sticky notes and photos. Ignacia scanned the images and was glad she didn't recognize any faces. It wouldn't have been a surprise to see one of her neighbors up there.

"Sit down. We've identified the victim as Michael Rotoni, a member of the 5th Street Gang. We haven't identified the shooter or motive."

Irene nodded. "You realize Agnes and I were the ones who found him, right? We have some new information, which may or may not be related to this."

"Go on." Sammy leaned in and rested her folded hands on the desk.

"I told Mother that he wasn't dead when they found him. At first, we thought he was, but when I tried to feel for his pulse, he moved his arm. And then he blinked. And then he said to find the cube."

"Well, that must have been a bit unsettling. Do you know anything about a cube?"

"Not really. I can ask the girls. Did you know there's a group of men who live in the house behind ours? We've encountered them a number of times. I have to say, they're a little on the shady side." Ignacia's eyes flipped to the ceiling as she shared about Bunny Slippers stealing the van, Joey and Smols at the door when they returned from Hope House saying we had something of theirs, and the vandalism which had to have been them.

"Well, that adds another layer, doesn't it?"

"One of them, Joey Lagratto, said he had been in a heist with a former gang. Maybe you know him? His little brother Robbie had followed him and had been shot in the process. Joey went to jail and now that he's out, wants to know where his little brother is buried."

Sammy's fingers clicked on the keyboard as she searched her database. She motioned Ignacia to her side, where they watched images scroll across the screen.

"That one—Ignacia pointed to the man, easily identifiable by the vines tattooed on his neck. "That's Joey."

Charges of larceny, grand theft auto, breaking and entering, and fraud.

"Does it show the name of the gang he was in?" Sammy scrolled down, reading through the lengthy list.

"5th Street Gang." She looked up where their eyes met.

13

Joey's bleary eyes checked the red light on his alarm clock. It was three a.m., and he was still awake, tossing and turning. His mind wouldn't stop whirring around like the rusty playground merry-go-round he had played on with Robbie as a kid. He had to get all the details straight if they were going to pull off the gold heist. Breaking into Big Red's house would be infinitely easier than the original heist. There wouldn't be a vault to break into, or guards to avoid.

If he stationed Squirt in the getaway van, G-man would check the recordings from the mics and cameras he had placed there earlier. Then Smols could load the chest onto the cart. Rosie nosed Joey's chin. He ran his hand down her head and back. How was he going to roll the cart down the stairs? It would certainly be too heavy to carry. Smols was strong, but this was way beyond his capabilities. Maybe he should have Bernardo bring the ramps. They should go through the backyard—no need to alert the neighbors.

He tossed himself to the other side, pulling the covers tightly around him. He supposed one way would be to have the men create a bucket brigade, passing the bars from one man to the next to the back porch until the chest was light enough to carry. No, that would probably take way too much time.

The light of the full moon shone through the cracked window of his room, creating a jagged shadow on the floor. If they did this at night, they would have to wait a few weeks until the moon was only a sliver. Could they make it happen during the day? Perhaps they could get up early, really early, like eight a.m. and pull it off while people were leaving for work and wouldn't notice them.

Joey had to listen to the recordings again. Make sure which day they were really planning to be gone. There was no room for mistakes. Not this time. Joey closed his eyes and tried to relax each part of his body—his face, his shoulders. His breath slowed.

Then he had it—it was almost Christmas, right? They could dress up as Santa and elves. It would be brilliant.

BERNARDO TURNED his jeep left at the corner onto Shepherd St. and 13th. Who knew that he would end up living in Joey's house only a few blocks from Marie's—the house that had actually been theirs together before he screwed up. He'd been able to fix a few things after his windfall from his *electrician* job—one of those being his jeep. That had worked out in his favor, for sure. Maybe it wouldn't hurt to pursue a repeat job. Probably would be better in another neighborhood. Then again, maybe Mr. Nice-guy would have recommended him to a few friends and neighbors.

Bernardo parked on the street in front of the house where Marie was outside hauling a ladder to the front. He jumped out of the jeep.

"Hey, let me help you with that." He took the back end and

followed her. It was nice of her to allow him into her life again. That's not to say everything was peaches and cream by any means. But there was an opening to work on their relationship. And if he played his cards right, they'd be back together by Christmas.

"Thanks. Let's put it up here. I want to put Christmas lights up. Amelia's been begging and begging."

"Well, we can't disappoint our little girl." It warmed him to use the word *our*.

Marie hauled a tub of lights from the garage. Bernardo took it from her, allowing his hands to touch hers. She didn't pull back. That was a good sign.

"Where is Amelia, anyway? I would think she'd be out here trying to help."

"She's with my mom. Spending a little grandma time going to see Santa. And truth be told, I needed a break. But she'll be excited when she comes home and sees the lights."

Bernardo laid the lights out on the grass and plugged them in to check the bulbs.

"I hope she comes home with pictures."

"I'm sure she will. You know my mom—now that she finally got rid of that flip phone and can take photos. That's all she does." Marie shrugged. "I think she's worried that Amelia's medicine will run out and she'll lose her."

Bernardo put his arm around her shoulders. "We're not gonna let that happen. I've been looking for jobs. I even stopped in at the trade school to see about being an electrician. They think I might be able to get a scholarship. I'm keeping my fingers crossed." She didn't need to know this was all just a thought in his head and he hadn't taken any action on it yet.

"Really? That would be good. But it would be a while before you earned any money, right?"

"Maybe, but I think that as an intern, I would get paid."

Marie turned and wrapped her arms around him and planted a kiss on his cheek. "Baby, I'm so proud of you." She beamed.

MORNING CHAPEL WAS OVER. Ignacia and Agnes walked down the cobbled path to the convent, the clear blue sky above illuminating shades of red in the fall leaves. Ignacia towered above Agnes—a good six inches over her four-foot-ten.

"I can't stop thinking about the basement."

"And the dead body?" Ignacia nodded.

"Who do you think killed him? Who was he? Why was he there? How did he get there?"

"Those are very good questions. Sammy and I haven't explored the basement again. I want to return and snoop around. There must be some clues." Ignacia gave Sammy a quick call to see if she was free.

Mama J stood at the back door of the convent. "Sister Ignacia and Agnes, you remember you're on bathroom cleaning duty while we're gone. We'll return in a few hours. That shouldn't take all day, so could you organize the kitchen too while we're at Hope House."

"We'd be glad to. Have fun. Say hi to the kids." Agnes smiled.

"By the way, Sammy is coming over so we can check out the basement again. Hopefully, we can gain some clues about how Michael and the shooter got in."

"That would be good. Let me know what you find out." Mama J closed the door behind her.

Not long after, Sammy arrived.

"Grab the emergency lanterns; it's dark down there." Ignacia slid the shelf back. "And grab some rags and a broom. Let's get some of those cobwebs out of the way." Ignacia and Agnes led Sammy down to the basement one slow step at a time.

"I can't unsee Mr. Deadman lying there when the police came." Agnes made the sign of the cross and held onto Ignacia's skirt.

They reached the bottom and swept their lights across the cement floor and over the cinder block walls of the musty room.

"Someone scrubbed the floor—there's just a faint sign of blood. The chalk outline of his body is still there," Agnes said.

"That was our crew. It wouldn't do to leave that vivid reminder." Sammy shone her light over the area. Just a clean spot and wheel tracks from the gurney were in the middle of the dusty floor.

Agnes extended the broom as high as she could reach, which wasn't far, and swiped at cobwebs. She jumped to reach the higher ones.

A spider clung to a web and landed on her shoulder. Agnes shrieked, dropping the broom, which clattered on the floor. Her eyes were wide as she swatted it. She wrapped her arms around her chest and shivered.

"It's just a little spider. Surely, you're not afraid of that." Ignacia frowned and shook her head.

"I know. I was just startled. I'm freezing. Aren't you cold?"

"A little. But we can't give up yet. Why don't you go back up and clean the kitchen? Sammy and I will keep searching."

Agnes nodded and left.

"Let's go systematically along the walls and look for any signs of another door or any way Mr. Deadman could have gotten in here." Sammy slowly shone her light from the top of the wall, stone by stone, to the floor.

They sidestepped and continued around the room. Ignacia felt the rough surface, examining the cement mortar for cracks or loose stones. Though there were spots where the mortar was worn, nothing was loose.

"Well, that did us a lot of good." Ignacia brushed her hands off on her apron. She'd have to change and wash it when they went back. "We haven't explored behind the shelves yet."

The shelves were heavy, by the looks of them, made from hand-hewn wood. They must have sat there since before Noah built the ark. Sammy set her hands on the back shelf and tried to pull while Ignacia shoved her shoulder into the opposite side. It didn't budge.

"We might have to remove all the canning jars. It's way too heavy." Sammy wiped sweat off her brow under her bangs.

"Do you really think we should take all those canning jars off? I mean, think about it. If it's this heavy to move, I can't see the culprit chasing the victim through an opening behind them. It would take too long."

"Yeah, I suppose you're right. But let's move the boxes. "She shone her light around the floor surrounding them. "I don't see any footprints or any sign of boxes sliding, do you?"

Ignacia knelt to get a closer look. "No, but still, it wouldn't hurt to move them and be sure there's not an opening behind them."

The boxes, although heavy enough to hold something, were easy to lift. Ignacia wanted to look inside, but Sammy was on a time frame. She'd return at another time. As they moved the final box next to the wall, a mouse skittered out. She was glad Agnes hadn't been there, or all heck would break loose.

Still, there was no sign of anything but stones and mortar.

"Okay, well, we haven't gone over the floor." Sammy checked her watch. They had already been down there for an hour—she needed to return to the office before too long.

"Maybe we should check the ceiling instead." Ignacia raised her eyebrows.

The beams revealed a ceiling that was constructed of exposed joists and rustic beams.

Old-growth fir was both the basement ceiling and the house floor.

Ignacia made mental calculations, something she knew she was gifted at. She never understood how others couldn't come to the same quick conclusions she did. Each beam was roughly ten inches by twelve. She measured the length of the room in steps. Just as she thought—fifteen feet long. She turned and repeated her stride—twenty feet wide. She stopped and put her finger to her lip as her eyes found the corner of the ceiling.

"This doesn't add up. It can't be right."

"Why?"

"Because our house is five hundred square feet. This isn't the full basement. It measures only three hundred square feet."

14

A MAP of Big Red's house was spread out on the worn carpet of Joey's house. Each of the men encircled it with Joey on his knees pointing out the plan. The time had come. They now knew when the house would be vacant and for how long.

"Okay, boys, this is what we're gonna do. G-man, you're sure that they'll all be outta the house day after tomorrow?"

He nodded.

"How long do you think they'll be gone?"

"They said they were taking the train to Baltimore to some kinda swap meet." G-man rolled his eyes. "No telling what kind of shenanigans they're planning. Anyway, they said they'd catch the train at ten, and it's almost a two-hour trip. I would venture they'd be gone at least four hours."

Joey lifted Rosie onto his lap. "Then we plan to be in and outta there in three hours or less."

Smols dropped a piece of lettuce in front of his tortoise, which moved one slow foot after another towards it.

"We better make it two and a half. I think we can do it. G-man, you've been there, what do you think?"

He rubbed his chin with his thumb and forefinger. "Yeah, I

mean, it's not that far from the living room to the backyard gate. You gotta watch out for that dang Rottweiler. He'll bark his head off and scare the snot outta you."

"Squirt, you'll drive. And this time, pay attention to the directions, ya got it? We won't have time for mess-ups." Squirt nodded his head and popped a ping pong ball up and down.

"Put that thing down!" Joey shook his head. Was he really gonna be able to get these guys all on the same page? Jeez.

Slingshot watched as a rat stood, scoping out his environs before he ran behind a shelf. Waiting for it to sneak out, Slingshot pulled his slingshot from his hip pocket, set a small stone into the pouch, took aim and in less than two seconds, hit the rat square between the eyes. He nodded his head in humble satisfaction. Rosie ran to the dead rat and sniffed, then backed up, turned and ran back to Joey.

"Hey! Quit yer foolin' around. We've got important work to do."

"That *was* important. You don't want that cute little rat crawling into your bed tonight, do you?"

"We're gonna use your skills. You'll be the watchman at the back door. Keep on the ready. And don't get distracted by birds and such. Ain't got time for that."

Slingshot nodded.

"Smols, I want you to be a distraction in the front yard. Decorate it with large candy canes, some lights. And find something like a blowup Grinch or something from Nightmare Before Christmas. Bystanders can watch you and not us."

Smols nodded. "Got it."

"Now for Bernardo—I hear you know a little bit about electricity. When you get done picking the lock to the back door, you can check the breaker box and make sure the lights don't pop it."

Joey looked around the room. "G-man, while Squirt is driving, you take the laptop and whatever you need to check the surveillance, so everything is cope, copset," he shook his head.

"Copesetic," Smols said, helping him out.

"What does that even mean?" Squirt tilted his head.

Slingshot swatted his shoulder with the back of his hand. "Dumb bell, it means everthin' is figured out. Don't you know nuthin'?"

"One more thing—Smols will be dressed in a Santa suit and the rest of you'll dress up as elves. But instead of leaving gifts, we'll help ourselves to some."

"How's it going with the investigation, Ignacia?" Mama J poured two cups of coffee and handed one to Irene.

"It's interesting, for sure. Mr. Deadman's name is Michael Rotoni."

Mama J crossed herself. "Have mercy on his soul."

"Also, we found out that Joey was in the same gang as Michael was—The 5th Street Gang. So, there must be some connection."

"You don't think Joey would have shot him? Or someone from that house?" And to think they had been over there. And what's more, those guys had been at Brother Ben's. Lordy, was this a good idea? Getting involved and letting them get involved with the children?

"That's what we're trying to figure out." Ignacia took a sip of her coffee. "There's one other question we need to answer. Before Michael died, he eked out something about finding a cube. Does that make any sense to you?"

Mama J took a long breath. "It sure does. Remember that bag of toys that was in the van? There was a Rubik's Cube in there.

Then, when we were cleaning up the vandalism, Ivan found it. He was all excited because he said Tony told him to look for it, and if he found it, he'd give him a soccer ball. I talked him into letting me keep the cube safe for him. Then Edith and I were deep in conversation, and she was nervously fiddling with it. She twisted it until it was the same color on each side, and it broke in two in her hands. Inside, would you believe it, was a small thumb drive."

"Ahhhhh." Ignacia put her fisted hand to her chin and nodded her head. "Now that makes a lot of sense. Do you have any idea what's on it? I mean, you still have it, right?"

"No, I mean yes, I mean, no, I don't know what's on it, and no, I gave it to Joey."

"You gave it to him? Why'd you do that?" Ignacia frowned.

She shook her head. "It seemed like the right thing to do at the time.

"Okay then. But I'm going to tell Sammy about it. I can't leave her out of the loop."

"Okay boys, this is the day. Time's a tickin'. We only have ninety minutes to get in and out of Big Red's humble abode before they return. Let's get this heist over and done with. Get your costumes on and hustle your heinies to the van."

Joey had been waiting long enough for this. He barely slept a wink the night before, playing and replaying the moves they would take. This had to go smoothly. And what a day of rejoicing it would be when they hauled off their loot. It brought a smile to his lips.

Smols, dressed in a full Santa suit, stood at the back door holding his phone, looking at his checklist. A pile of elf hats sat on the counter beside him.

"David, you got your slingshot? Just in case?" Slingshot nodded. Smols placed an elf hat on his head.

Smols glanced first at Bernardo's tool bag, then at his slippers. "Bernardo, do you have to wear those dumb slippers?"

Bernardo sneered at Smols. Those slippers were almost magic. Not only were they comfortable, but it seemed a lot of things went right when he wore them. And besides, they had been a gift from Amelia. So, what the heck.

"Do you have what you need to pick the locks?" He handed him an elf hat.

He held up a pick. "I've got wire cutters and some other tools if I need to monkey with the electricity."

Smols erased items on the list as each person passed.

G-Man held up his laptop. His earbuds hung around his neck. Smols handed him an elf hat. "I ain't wearing that thing."

"Have to. The boss says."

"It's stupid."

Joey walked up and smacked G-man across the back of his head. G-Man slid it on without comment. Rosie jumped on Joey's leg, begging to go.

"Not this time. You'd spoil everything."

Rosie whined. "We'll be back soon. Go lie down." She took a few steps, turned and pleaded. Joey pointed his finger towards the bed, and Rosie slunk off.

Loaded into the van, Joey asked, "Where's Squirt?"

"He was here a few minutes ago. Then he left." David looked out the tinted window. He shrugged.

Squirt came running and slid into the driver's seat. "Sorry, I lost the key." He held it up. "It was buried under a bunch of socks in my drawer." He shrugged and started the van.

15

Tim Hansen, from forensics, walked into Sammy Jerard's office holding a Ziplock baggie with the Michael Rotoni mystery. Sammy turned away from her computer screen.

"Look what we found."

"The bullet? Did you figure out what type of gun?"

Tim shook his head. "Nope. It's weird, but there was no sign of a bullet."

"What?"

"I know. But what I did find was traces of grass and bits of dirt on his shoes."

Sammy shook her head. Anyone could have figured that out. "That doesn't help much. He had to have come in from outside, so unless he went from a vehicle to the asphalt to the sidewalk to the house, there would be grass and dirt." It didn't take a forensic to figure that out.

"True, but the next step is to determine if it matches the grass at the convent. What were you working on before I came in?" Tim leaned against the edge of the desk and crossed his legs at the ankles. The sleeves of his green button-down shirt were rolled up to just below his elbows, exposing muscled forearms and a tattoo of a chameleon.

Sammy slid a glance at his arms and quickly switched her screen back to a plot map of the 1300 block of Quincy Street, where the convent was located. She enlarged the image, set to Google Earth.

"Trying to get the lay of the land. This is the convent. When Sister Ignacia and I explored the basement where Michael was found, she paced out the dimensions of the basement. It measured twenty-four feet. She was puzzled because that didn't match the size of the house. It was way smaller."

"There's a house right behind it. What do you know about it?"

"Not much." Sammy brought up another screen with a 3-D image of the convent floor plan. Tim scooted a chair next to Sammy's. It showed the front door, facing the street, the large living room that filled the downstairs, with the massive kitchen adjacent. She enlarged the image and pointed.

"Look, there's the staircase going down to the basement, with the basement under the kitchen and living room. Ignacia swore by the size." Sammy enabled the ruler guide.

"She was right." Tim pointed, letting his shoulder brush Sammy's. "The entire basement indeed has a wider footprint. See this line? There must be an additional ten feet beyond their wall."

Sammy turned. "So somewhere there has to be an opening. We searched high and low and found nothing. No windows. No doors." She wrinkled her brow. "What do you make of this?"

"May I?" Tim took the mouse. "Let's see what's behind the convent." A few clicks later revealed the yard of the old house. That house is further back from the perimeter of the basement. The yard is way larger than what appears to be the total space of the additional basement."

"What year do you think these old houses were built?" Sammy pulled her long blonde hair and twisted it into a bun on top of her head. She tucked the ends under the bun and poked a pencil through it to hold it in place.

Tim did a quick search. "Had to have been around 1850–60s. That would have been around the Civil War."

"When there would have been slaves. Perhaps this was built as a hiding place."

"They would probably have had root cellars too, which the basement might have served as."

Sammy sat back in her leather office chair and crossed her arms. "So, you're suggesting that there's an entrance to the back basement, which had a hidden door to the convent basement." Tim nodded. Sammy stood and gave him an exuberant hug.

"Dinner tonight?"

How could she resist the dimples that dotted his cheeks and those deep green penetrating eyes? He may not be the smartest cookie in the batch, but still felt the warmth of his shoulder and, wise or not, she nodded.

8:02 am

A white panel van with a vinyl sign that said *Santa's Helpers* pulled up in front of Big Red's house. It had been a huge stretch to get everyone up and moving that early in the morning. A large spruce towered over them in the yard. The early morning winter sun was just peeking over the roofs of the houses on the east side casting the tree's shadow onto the brownstone walls of the house.

True to G-Man's report, there was no sign of anyone around. He turned in the van to make eye contact with the others.

"Okay, we've got exactly one hundred twenty minutes. That's

two hours for those of you who can't tell time. So, let's get in and get out."

Two elves, a 6'5" Santa and Joey jumped out. G-Man remained in the van with the computer for surveillance. As soon as they unloaded the large candy canes, the giant inflatable Oogie Boogie and other paraphernalia, Squirt took off to park in the back alley.

Smols positioned the candy canes first along the perimeter of the sidewalk. He stood back observing the placement. Satisfied, he nodded his head. Next, he positioned Oogie Boogie opposite the spruce tree where there would be adequate room. The neighbor, who himself had the blowup Santa and Frosty was walking his corgi. He wore a long plaid scarf covering the buttons on his tan wool coat. His head was covered with a hand-knit navy blue hat. He stopped in front of Big Red's yard and watched as Smols began to set up the decoration.

"Hey, I'm Bill, the neighbor. It's nice to see something positive going on here."

Smols turned and put on a large grin. "That's what Santa does—always something nice. It seemed like the residents here could use a little Christmas cheer."

"I'd sure agree with that. Wait, are they even around?" He glanced at the window. "I can't imagine them letting you do this."

"My elves say they'll be gone for a bit. Just wanted to give them a little surprise."

The corgi barked. "Hush now." Bill reached down and petted him. "Can I give you a hand? I'm pretty good at these things."

BACK IN THE VAN, G-Man set his walkie talkie beside him and cued up his computer to the camera feed. He whispered into his walkie talkie to Joey. "Man in front helping Smols. Shut off any lights and make sure the curtains are closed."

Squirt jumped out of the van and walked through the back gate—the same one G-Man had gone through to set up the cameras. Right on cue, the Rottweiler behind the fence on the right began barking. Even knowing that would happen, Squirt jumped. *Just keep walking. He'll quit in a minute.* Squirt took the back steps, watching for the loose board, glanced over his shoulder and tried the door.

It was still locked. He peered in the window but didn't see anyone. Squirt wrapped his arms around himself and jumped up and down to keep warm. The elf costume might have been cute, but it certainly wasn't warm.

On the front porch, Bernardo pulled out his pic and made short work of the lock. The door squeaked open, and Joey, Tony, Slingshot and Bernardo moved in. Bernardo heard rapping on the back door and hustled to open it for Squirt. Joey pulled out the walkie talkie to alert G-Man that all were inside.

The chest remained in the same spot they had seen from the camera footage, complete with the doily covering and fake flowers in a vase on top. Joey rubbed his hands together. This was too good to be true.

"Okay men, let's make this quick. Here's the chest. Each of you fill your backpack with as many bars as you can carry." He lifted the lid and let out a whistle. Inside were gold bars, alright. But it seemed a site less than what showed on the big screen. Instead of being filled to the top, only eight bars remained. Joey's jaw dropped. "Son of a rotten banana!"

MEANWHILE, G-Man figured he didn't need to watch surveillance anymore. He wanted to snoop around the house. Get access to their computer. What other clues to advantage could he uncover? With his own laptop under his arm, he jumped out of the van and into the back door of the house, left ajar by Squirt. The others stood in a semi-circle around the chest. He walked behind them and upstairs to the room where he had seen the computer the last time he was there.

A large mahogany desk sat with two upholstered rolling chairs. A computer with two additional 22" large screen monitors filled most of the desk. He wiggled the mouse, and it came to life. Within minutes, and a few strokes, he hacked into it. There weren't many folders on the desktop, but one in particular stood out. The one labeled crypto. G-Man clicked on it. Trading wins, wallet addresses, trading strategies. He whooshed out a low whistle.

"Joey, get your arse up here. You've got to see this!"

"Wait. I'm in the middle of something."

8:23 a.m.

G-man checked the time. "We don't have all day, and you are not going to want to miss this." While G-man waited, he air-dropped the files to his computer. What kind of idiot was Big Red not to have 2-step verification? He must be pretty cocky.

SMOLS OPENED the box for the Oogie Boogie and attached the power cord to the inflatable. Bernardo had eyed him from inside and hustled out to help him. It didn't take him long to discover an outside outlet, into which he plugged an extension cord. He handed the female end to Smols who plugged in his cord. No power. Bernardo slapped his palm to his forehead and ran inside, searching for the breaker box. Not in the middle of the hall. Not in the kitchen. He was certain it wouldn't be located upstairs. He took the stairs two at a time, from the kitchen to the basement. It had to be there.

Sure enough, it was. But that was not all that was there. The basement was filled with thirty ANT Miners. Holy moly! They were mining cryptocurrency. Besides the gold bars, they had their fingers in something worth as much or more than those. Well, he'd just have to do something about it. Their goal today was to clean them out. And that's just what he was about to do.

16

THE CLOUDLESS DECEMBER air was brisk, and frost sparkled on the sidewalk. Ignacia pulled a knit scarf tighter around her neck and slipped on the fur-lined mittens her mom had knit for her. There were a few remaining fall leaves on the ground, their colors fading as they decomposed into the yards. Christmas lights adorned fences and gutters, their twinkling making things looks cheery.

"Sammy, let's review what we know so far. A man, Michael Rotoni, was shot through the chest. No bullet was found." Ignacia's rosary beads bounced on her leg as she walked.

Sammy nodded. "We also know that Joey Lagrotto was in the 5th Street Gang along with our buddy Mikey."

"Maybe. Maybe not. They for sure were in the same gang, but we don't know for certain if it was at the same time." Ignacia pointed out an inflatable snowman and Santa in the yard as they passed by. Giant candy canes bordered the next yard and held an inflatable Oogie Boogie.

"Yeah, you're right. We now know that the convent basement extends beyond the perimeter of the house. And that the house was built at the time of slavery. Which leads us to believe there may be a connecting entrance and possible history of hiding slaves by abolitionists."

"So, we need to search again for the entrance." Sammy nodded.

Ignacia continued. "And we need to find the motive and the killer."

"Maybe we need to check for evidence again. A bullet isn't enough. There has to be some other clue." Sammy shoved her hands in her coat pockets. "Let's head back and check out the basement once more."

THE CHILDREN, dressed in their jammies, sat on the carpet in front of the fireplace. Yellow and orange flames licked the logs, occasionally emitting sparks, which especially pleased the girls. It was magical. Brother Ben sat in a wooden rocking chair with his large Bible in his lap. "Children, do you know why I believe in God?"

Mykita and Olena nodded their heads.

"Why do you think?" he continued.

"Because he made us." Olena's blue eyes sparkled.

"And he loves you." Mykita stroked her long braid.

Liliya put her arm around Mykita. "He loves you too. He loves everybody."

"Well, he doesn't love me." Ivan's head sunk and he wrapped his arms around his middle.

"Does so," Liliya said. "He even loves you when you're a brat."

Brother Ben raised a warning finger and shook his head.

"Let's see what the Bible says about God." He put on his glasses, opened it and turned a few pages. "Here we are— Psalm 38 says, the Lord is close to the brokenhearted and saves those who are crushed in spirit. What do you suppose that means—crushed in spirit?"

Taras raised his hand. "It means your heart feels smooshed. You don't have any energy because you're hurting."

"That's a good way of putting it. So, let's talk about that. Put your hand on your heart if you're feeling crushed in spirit." Brother Ben looked at each child in turn. Each had his or her hand placed on his or her chest. Each of them was broken.

"Tell me what worries you, Ivan." He shook his head, barely a move. "We can come back to you later. What about you, Bohdan?"

"I'm afraid I'll never see my parents again." Others nodded. Mykita's eyes teared up.

"Me too. Or my big brother."

"I don't know if my grandma is okay. She was living alone, and a bomb blew up her barn. It was so scary." Vova's shoulders raised to his ears.

"What if my family doesn't have enough to eat?" Taras shrugged. "The grocery stores were being raided before we were put on the boat to come here. Maybe there isn't any food."

Brother Ben closed his eyes. *Lord, thank you for bringing me these children. I can't begin to tell you how much they have blessed me. Your word says to defend the weak and fatherless; uphold the cause of the poor and oppressed. Rescue the weak and needy and deliver them from the hand of the wicked. Continue to guide me.*

He made the sign of the cross and looked up. He turned a few more pages in his Bible.

"Children, I want to read one more verse to you. And then I have something special for you."

"What is it?"

"Be patient. This verse is in Isaiah. *So do not fear, for I am with you; do not be discouraged, for I am your God. I will strengthen you and help you; I will hold onto you with my righteous right hand.*

Now isn't that something? The very same God who created the earth and skies and all living creatures, the one who created you, cares about each of you. And he says, don't worry. Don't fear. I will be with you."

Brother Ben picked up a manila envelope from the floor. He held it between his thumbs and forefingers for them to see.

"What is it?"

"Can we see?"

"Is it for us?" chorused off the stones of the fireplace.

"This should strengthen you." He smiled as he pulled out a dozen letters from the envelope.

The children ran to him. "Are they for us?"

"Yes, they are for you. From your parents. Now isn't this just about the nicest present you could ever have?" Brother Ben grinned from ear to ear and began calling names.

"Taras, could you help Vova with his? Read it to him?"

Taras took Volva's little three-year-old hand, and they walked to the couch and sat down.

"Here's yours, Ivan." Ben held it out to him. Ivan grabbed for it and Ben snatched it back. Ivan turned and stomped his feet. "Come here, I'm just playing with you."

"It's *not* funny!"

Ben gave him his letter and put his arm around him "I'm sorry. You're right. It wasn't funny."

Brother Ben passed out the rest of the letters. The girls made a circle on the floor and took turns hearing each read their letters aloud.

Last was Bohdan. He handed his letter to him, complete with a hand-drawn picture of a snowman on the envelope. The eight-year-old's blonde hair spiked up. His new front teeth were too large for his mouth, but his smile was as large as a crescent moon.

Ben stood, placing his hands on his hips. He ran his hand through his beard and smiled as he heard snatches of voices.

"I miss you so, so much, my darling. It's very cold here. I'm sure you're more comfortable at Hope House. Please write to us."

"...tried to milk the cow but his fingers were frozen..."

"...so glad you are safe with Brother Ben. I hope you have new friends."

"...a little gift for you. It's not much, but a lock of hair should remind you of me."

The letters had been smuggled out of the country, probably written months ago. But by God's grace, they had arrived safely. There was nothing that could bring more hope, than hearing from their families.

17

8:49 am

Bernardo opened the electrical panel, dug in his tool bag and pulled out the wire nippers. He knew these would come in handy. And what do you know? Each of the breakers were labeled.

Washing machine, dryer, kitchen, basement. Yes, the basement! He shut off the main. Smols would be wondering what the heck was taking him. This should only take a minute, though, if everything went the way it was supposed to. A little prayer from those nun girls could be helpful right about now.

Next, he unscrewed the metal panel covering the branch wires, their reds, blacks and greens twisted and running amuck. Having actually started his electrician internship, he had learned enough to do this important job. Marie would be proud of him. He straightened his shoulders. Proud that he had an internship. This job? This wasn't something he planned to share with her.

Fitting the cable cutter onto the wires leading to the basement breaker, he snipped and the wires fell into two. The humming and blinking of the ANT Miners abruptly stopped.

Bernardo may as well snip the wire to the basement lights as well. That would throw them bad boys for a loop, too. He smiled, turned on the main beakers, and replaced the cover. Hustling up the steps, he sprang onto the main floor and out the front door.

"Give it a try." Bernardo adjusted his elf hat and feigned a smile at the neighbor.

"You guys really know how to pull off a good surprise. Hey, I know a couple other neighbors who might like this kind of Christmas gift too. Want me to tell you where they live?"

"Now aren't you a great neighbor. Thanks, but we've got a pretty long list already."

8:55 am

Inside, Joey adjusted his fedora. "What do you 'spose they did with the other gold?"

"You don't think they knew we were comin'?" David pulled his slingshot from his hip pocket ready for action. He twirled it around his finger.

From upstairs, G-man hollered, "Joey, hurry up." The analog clock hand on the wall ticked. Only forty-five more minutes left until the end of the safe zone. G-man was getting impatient, and he couldn't stop his leg from bouncing up and down.

"I don't know. Squirt, Slingshot, Tony—dig in. Each bar is about twenty-seven pounds, so you should be able to take three each and still be spry. Get a move on!" Then Joey headed to the stairs.

Squirt slapped Slingshot on the back. "Dig in." He laughed. "Get it? Gold diggers?"

Tony pulled out three bars and placed them in his pack. Squirt pulled out two and lifted them over his head like weights.

Slingshot laughed and reached for his three, handing Squirt his last one.

"There are only two left. How can that be? You told us each to take three, Boss." He looked puzzled.

"That's cuz he's only got a fourth-grade education. He didn't learn his division facts," Tony said. He looked over his shoulder for Joey. "Hustle, Zip up and head to the van."

9:04 am

"Listen, Bill, glad for your help. We've gotta skedaddle to get to our next place." Smols took the cardboard box the inflatables were in and flattened it.

"Want me to put that in my recycle bin for you?" Bill reached for it.

Smols handed it over. "You're on the nice list, Bill." He winked. Bill walked off wearing a huge grin and a spring in his step.

Bill leaned down to his corgi, took its ears in his hands and said, "Did you hear that? I'm on the nice list!"

Bernardo and Smols watched Bill return to his house.

HEARING THE FRONT DOOR CLOSE, Joey said, "They're gone. Now we can concentrate."

G-Man checked the time. "Yeah, well, we've only got twenty-six minutes in our safe zone. Look here," he pointed to the desktop. There are three folders—they're all crypto files."

"Open the Coin Based Trading Wins. That should give us an idea of what they're into." Joey leaned in. "Wow, they're making 100s of percents. Look at this."

"Yeah," G-Man said, "but they're using leverage. That could ruin us in seconds."

"Whoa. The Bitcoin market has been pumping this week. Keep hearing people make thousands—we should trade this crypto and retire."

Joey's mind went to Robbie. If they could find his body, this would pay for a proper casket and burial.

"We don't have time. Stick to the plan," G-Man said.

"What about the Trading Strategies? Pull them up." Joey's fingers tapped the desk.

G-Man ignored him and slid the folder to the left monitor.

Joey stopped tapping. "Oh," he patted his shirt pocket, "Mama J gave me this little piece of heaven." He pulled out the thumb drive, and handed it to G-Man.

G-Man leapt, totally uncharacteristic of his usual behavior.

"Do you know what this is, Man?" He kissed it.

"Some weird type of thumb drive."

G-Man inserted the Ledger Nano X into the USB slot on the computer.

"This thing is no ordinary thumb drive. It's a crypto hardware wallet." His leg bounced faster as he clicked, waiting for it to appear. A message asking for the password appeared.

"Great. Now what?"

G-Man closed his eyes trying to envision what it could be. He opened them, and typed a few random characters. No luck.

"It takes twenty-six characters that are a combo of pretty much everything on the keyboard. We may not be able to get in."

"Come on, G-Man. You can figure this out. You're a techno-wizard." Joey patted his back.

Joey scanned the desk and, finding nothing, opened the desk drawer. There on top was a notebook. "Take a look at this. Maybe there's a clue."

G-Man opened it. "What do you know, the first page contains crypto login passwords."

He smiled as he attempted logging in with the first one. It failed. "Read these stupid symbols to me. I must have gotten them wrong."

Joey read ten symbols and squinted his eyes. "I can't read this. Here, you look at it."

G-Man tried to read it, but it was smudged. "There's more, right? Read the next one. Maybe they had to create a new password."

Joey began reading them off again as G-Man typed.

Login Failed.

G-Man leaned back in his chair and locked his hands behind his head. He breathed a square—one breath in, turn the corner, one breath out, turn the corner, one in, turn, one out.

"We can't get this wrong! If we don't login now, we'll never get access."

"Okay, Mr. Know-it-all. Go ahead. But if you fail, this whole heist is on your plate."

"There's one more password. It says crypto hardware wallet. Here goes nothing."

Holy Smokes—it opened. There were multiple wallet names with addresses associated with them. $BTC, $ETH, $DOGE.

"Perfect timing. Right in the middle of the biggest crypto market pump to date!" Joey slapped G-Man's hand.

10:30 am

"There's 3,000- Bitcoin there. That's like thirty million dollars right now!" Joey was beside himself.

"Okay, let's withdraw it and get the hell out of here."

"We should trade this and make even more money." Joey couldn't contain the energy pulsing through his veins.

"No, we're sticking to the plan. You can worry about that later."

Joey took over and withdrew the bitcoin to his CashApp Bitcoin Wallet. He glanced at G-Man. "From what I understand, it's gonna take a few minutes for the miners to confirm the withdrawal on the blockchain. Should only take a few minutes."

"We have exactly three minutes and twenty seconds." G-Man closed the file folders while they waited. "They'll never recover from this."

They jumped as the front door slammed. What should they do? They didn't dare shut down the computer. They'd lose everything. Then again, if they were seconds away from getting caught, what would be the difference? They'd probably be dead.

18

10:45

Joey raced to shut the door. Heavy footsteps landed on the stairs, a step at a time. A rap at the door. Joey pulled a pistol from the back of his pants.

"Hey, it's Smols. Come on, the van's in front waiting."

Joey opened the door. "What the fudge!"

G-Man, with his head in the computer, said, "Okay, here we go. The withdrawal is confirmed."

He pulled the Nano from the computer, replaced the folders, and put it to sleep. He pulled a hanky from his hip pocket and wiped the keyboard and desk surfaces. Joey stuck his hand out, palm up.

G-Man dropped the Nano into it, and they hot-tailed it outta there.

As soon as Ignacia ushered Sammy into the convent, they were hit by the sweet fragrance of sugar and cinnamon. The sound of the mixer whirling lured them right into the kitchen, their noses in the air taking in every ounce of goodness.

"You're just in time. Do you want to help make sugar cookies? We thought we'd bring them to all our neighbors." Agnes held up a rubber spatula and licked the batter.

"Our back door neighbors won't be able to resist these. Teresa took two aprons from the hook and handed them to Sammy and Ignacia.

"We'd love to help, but we're on a mission to find how anyone got in and out of the basement. But maybe you could save us a few cookies?"

Sammy followed Ignacia to the pantry, but first they each dipped their fingers in the batter and popped them in their mouths.

"A mission? Did you say find? You know who you need to pray for, don't ya?" Agnes said, her mouth full of goodness.

"St. Anthony. The finder of lost things." Ignacia placed her hands together and raised them in prayer.

They started for the pantry.

"Uh, we just got an Uber delivery of a ton of groceries. It might take you a while to get to the door."

Irene pursed her lips. "Well, okay then." They found some empty crates and began loading cans of red beans, pumpkin, cranberry sauce, shortening, and loaves of bread.

"Ignacia, help me move this fifty-pound bag of flour." They slid it to the floor and laid it next to the wall. Next, they drug an equally large bag of sugar next to the flour. Twenty minutes later, when they heard the oven timer ding, they had filled ten crates, and the shelves were light enough to move.

"First batch of cookies is out, ladies. You sure you don't want to test them and see if they're edible?" Agnes smiled, slid two onto a metal spatula and offered them.

Sammy took one, bit into the warm gooeyness and nodded.

Igmacia took a bite of hers. "Nahhh, these are awful." She scrunched up her nose. "Nobody's going to want these." It didn't stop her from taking a second bite. And a third.

"Come on, let's go. My boss is gonna wonder what's taking so long. Besides, I've got to be back in time for a date." Sammy's face flushed.

Shoving with their shoulders, they moved the shelf out of the way. This time, they were prepared. They had gloves. And they had head lamps which they strapped on, and made their way down the old wooden steps, their right hands on the wall for balance. At the bottom, they shone the lights to the left. Sammy placed one in the center of the room tilted towards the ceiling. Ignacia set one on the floor to face the underside of the stairs.

"First things first." Ignacia grabbed Sammy's hand. "Let's pray." Sammy lifted her eyebrows. She wasn't sure praying was in her comfort zone.

Ignacia made the sign of the cross. "Jesus, you know the end of this mystery. Lead the way to your truth and while you're at it, bless those guys in the house behind us. Especially Joey. He seems to be the one in most need of your mercy." She let go of Sammy's hands.

"You prayed for Joey and that bunch of cons? Weren't they the ones that wrecked your van, vandalized your house and threatened you?"

"Yep, that's exactly why we want God to bless them. If He does, they'll turn from their wicked ways. Come on. We've got a door or something to find."

Ignacia said a silent prayer for Sammy too. Maybe if she spent enough time with her, Ignacia would rub off on her. Not that she had to become a sister or anything, but she could benefit from a little Jesus in her life.

The steps were supported by four hand-hewn twelve-inch

beams, which connected to the stringers on which the wooden steps were placed. Contrary to the rest of the walls, six-inch wood slats covered the wall under the steps. Instead of the space being empty, it had several old wooden crates, dusty and covered with cobwebs. In the middle, were green bottles of wine, corks screwed into the tops. No telling how old they were. They pulled everything away from the wall and examined it. Sammy picked up the work light and shone it. Nope. No sign of an entrance.

"What about under here?" Sammy said.

The last three feet at the foot of the stairs had a small plywood wall nailed to the stringers and beam.

"Let me crawl under and see what's there. You don't want to try and crawl around, Ignacia—your habit will be filthy."

Ignacia nodded, took the light and angled it into the dark space while Sammy ran her fingers over the boards, trying to find any opening.

"See anything?"

"Not yet. But something *has* to be there." They both jumped at a loud bang—almost like something heavy had been dropped.

"What was that?" Ignacia looked up to the kitchen door. It still stood open.

"I don't think it's from our house. It sounded like it was behind this wall." Sammy frowned. "Did you ever see anything outside? An outbuilding? Anything that might be connected?"

"No. But that doesn't mean something doesn't exist. Let's go outside and check things out." Was it safe? Would they meet someone out there? Someone they didn't really want to run into?

Sammy slid out and repositioned the tie in her hair to keep if from falling in her face. They ran up the stairs and into the kitchen.

"That was quick. Did you find it?" Teresa was wiping down

the counters with a rag and scooping leftover flour into the garbage.

Ignacia shook her head, grabbed another cookie and headed outside.

———

THE SKY HAD TURNED grey and tiny bits of snow drifted down looking like bits of white confetti. The weather had dropped below freezing, and as tiny flakes hit the ground they began to cover like manna in the wilderness. The sun, though obscured behind the clouds had moved below the horizon, causing the temperature to drop a few more degrees. The snow turned to larger flakes that covered Big Red's yard and the Christmas cheer that adorned it.

A deep red Mercedes G wagon slid into the driveway backwards, parked ready for a quick getaway if needed. The smoky tinted windows hid the five others from view. The four doors flung open and three men jumped out. Big Red took two steps towards the yard and stopped. He was an imposing figure. Not near as tall as Smols but muscled and stern. If he smiled, it was one of derision, not joy. A permanent scowl on his face caused the tattoo of his gang name on his bald forehead to wrinkle. Multiple chains around his neck adorned his chest, one with a large cross. Who knew why that was there. Did he think it would protect him from his sins?

"Sweet mother of all messy Mondays. Where did all this !@& come from?"

Moe's steps made prints in the snow as he moved towards the candy canes. He touched one, and a smile formed under his black mustache. Childhood memories whisked him away from his present life, if even for a moment. His black sweatshirt hood shadowed his face, preventing Big Red to notice.

George scowled as his eyes raised to the towering eight-foot Oogie Boogey.

"What kinda pranksters would have done this?"

"Move aside." Big Red aimed, and the rat-tat-tat-tat-tat of his machine gun echoed off the walls of the brownstone. Moe jumped as the candy canes fell one by one. Air whooshed out of the tall, cream-colored Oogie Boogie as he melted into the snow. Big Red nodded with satisfaction and climbed the steps to the front porch. He unlocked the door and switched on the light. Sweeping his eyes around the living room, he stepped inside. Nothing seemed amiss. The chest was in the same spot, with the tablecloth and flowers unmoved. Whoever had their little bit of fun must have kept it all outside.

19

SAMMY STEPPED out of the convent door, looked at the sky and shivered. She ran back in and got their coats. Ignacia followed, gingerly taking steps in snow that was going on five inches.

"It's freezing out here!" Sammy's coat wasn't as warm as she would have liked. "It's getting dark too. Are we going to be done in time for my date with Tim?"

"Maybe. Maybe not." Having a date wasn't anything Ignacia had experienced and never would. Getting nervous or excited about it might cause Sammy to miss clues. Ignacia would have to be more vigilant in her observations.

Sammy sent a quick text to Tim to meet her there. She returned her phone to her pocket and made her way a few steps until her feet slipped out from under her. She squealed as she fell on her bum.

"Sammy, what happened?"

"What do you think—it's pretty obvious." Sammy frowned.

"But why was it so slick there?" Ignacia held her hands out to Sammy to help her up.

Sammy brushed off her behind and looked at the ground where she slipped.

"That's not grass. Look." Sammy slid her foot over it. "It's metal. Did you know this was here?"

Ignacia shook her head, knelt and brushed the remaining snow from the two-foot square. "There's a handle." She slid her fingers under the icy depression and grasped the D-shaped handle. She tugged, but it didn't budge.

"Maybe it's frozen." Sammy tried the handle again, and it lifted.

"Where do you think this goes? Are you sure you never saw this before?"

"Nope. It's probably been covered with grass and weeds." How many times had Ignacia walked over this to go to chapel and never seen it?

Maybe this is what Sammy and Tim had seen on the map. Sammy took her phone from her pocket and shone the flashlight down the stone steps.

"Are we going in?"

Ignacia didn't answer but proceeded in.

"This must be a root cellar. Looks like we have a theme here, exploring underground dark places."

They reached the bottom where old crates were filled with potatoes, beets and what looked like carrots. How long they had been there was anyone's guess. The fact that they weren't growing eyes or rotting was cause for pause. Had someone put them here recently?

"All this is interesting, but what in the world made that sound? Remember, that's why we're here?" Ignacia said.

"Ignacia—" Mama J stood on the back porch and hollered. "Ignacia, where are you?"

Hearing her, Ignacia whooshed a sigh, and they retraced their steps and exited the cellar.

"I'm here. Do you need me?"

"Yes, I'm actually looking for Sammy. Her friend Tim is here. What are you ladies doing down there?"

THE GETAWAY VAN pulled up in front of Joey's home. Doors opened and slammed as the men carried their backpacks into the house. It wasn't but a few seconds later when red and blue lights swirled from a cop car pulling to the front of the house.

Joey's heart seized. "Let me take care of this, boys." He took his time opening the door. He just had to play it cool. It had worked before, and it could work again. His sneakers hit the porch. First, he straightened his posture and then his fedora. If there were ever a time he needed prayers, it was now.

The officer stepped out of his car and turned towards Joey.

"Officer Bradley, what an honor." Joey held out his hand, which the officer shook.

"Joey, my boy. I missed you at our scheduled meeting."

"Yeah, yeah. Why don't you come inside?" Joey put his hand on his shoulder and ushered him in.

"Have a seat. Make yourself comfortable. Can I offer you some cookies? They're fresh made from our neighbors. Smols, bring our friend here some cookies."

Bradley scanned the room. "Nice digs you got here, Joey. Could use a sweep and a prayer, though."

Smols handed Officer Bradley a paper towel with a few cookies, glanced at his badge and raised his eyebrows at Joey. He leaned his back against the wall and crossed his arms.

"Yeah, yeah. We been busy." *If he only knew.*

"Good cookies." Bradley held one up. "Too busy to show up at your parole meeting?"

Joey shifted. "About that. My ma broke her hip. I've been over there helping her. You probably know that my little bro was shot, so she only has me now." Joey shifted his eyes, looking contrite.

"I'm sorry about your mom. That's harsh. When did she fall? How did it happen?"

"Last week, Sir. It was on Thursday, right Smols?" Smols nodded. "She saw some purty little birds and wanted to take some pics of them. She went for her camera and, darned if she didn't slip on some spilt coffee. Ma was in a pretty bad way."

"Sounds like it was a good thing you were able to help her. Do you have any documentation? A doctor's note? Appointment schedule? Something? I'm not doubting you, but you know the rules."

"I'll be seeing her tonight. I'll see what I can round up for you."

"Joey, you can't go dark on me. If something comes up, you call, understand? Otherwise, it'll be a violation."

"Thank you, Sir. I won't miss again. I'm workin' hard at cleaning up my act."

Bradley nodded scanned the room once more and left. Joey watched until the car sped away, and they all breathed a sigh of relief.

Joey and the boys sat around the living room, their back-packs on the floor in front of them. Squirt came in with his arms loaded with beer. He tossed a can to each of them, then returned with a can of Squirt for himself. He sat on the arm of the same lounge chair Slingshot occupied. Slingshot removed his ball cap and threw it up in the air.

"Whooweeee! We did it!" A grin split his face and showed a few teeth that desperately needed dental work.

Even Joey smiled. Rosie licked the beer off his mouth. "Empty your bags and let's debrief the operation."

They pulled out the gold bars and stacked them in a

pyramid on the coffee table. They gleamed in contrast with the well-worn wood.

"I need everyone to fill me in on the deets that I didn't see. Start with Smols."

Smols nodded, took a swig of his beer and set it down. "When Bill, the neighbor came by, I thought he was gonna do us in. Fortunately, he was more than helpful. And I have to say, the yard looked pretty festive. We did have a little conundrum when the power didn't work."

Bernardo leaped in. "So, I searched for the breaker box and found it in the basement. Those nuns musta been praying for us, cuz you wouldn't believe what I found." A pregnant pause.

"Don't leave us in suspense, Dude." Squirt leaned in.

"The entire basement was full, and I mean *full* of ANT miners, humming and glowing." Bernardo looked at the puzzled faces surrounding him.

"Crypto—they're mining crypto. At least they were. So, I thought to myself, how can I interfere with their little project? I whipped out my trusty nippers and snipped all the wires leading to the basement. That beautiful sound of silence and no more blinking lights. It was glorious." He nodded.

"I guess I can add to that." G-Man leaned his elbows on his knees. "When I was there the first time, setting the cameras in place, I found their computer in the office upstairs. So, I took advantage of the time and scoped it out. Lucky for me, the idiots didn't have a password to get into it. I found a folder on the desktop with trading wins, wallet addresses, trading strategies. I air dropped them to my computer."

G-Man glanced at Joey, who gave a warning shake of his head. He wasn't ready to share the end of the story with them. Joey nonchalantly stroked his chin. "I bet they sold or traded the gold for crypto. I wonder why they didn't do it all?"

Tony laughed. "They wanted to share the wealth with us—you know, a sorta Christmas present."

"If you want, Boss, I can figure out a trade for the bars as well." G-man picked up a bar and fingered it.

"Okay, look into it."

A knock on the door startled them. They glanced at the window, and Rosie hopped off Joey's lap to run barking to the door. Smols answered, slowly pulling the knob and peeking out. Mama J, Ignacia and Agnes stood, faces of innocence, holding a large tray of fresh gingerbread cookies.

"Thank you, ladies. Let me take those off your hands." He turned his head and gave an exaggerated nod of warning. Joey grabbed the throw off the couch and covered the coffee table.

"Would you mind if we came in? We wanted to ask a favor." Mama J took a step forward.

20

Smols saw that the coast was clear and opened the door to Mama J, Ignacia and Agnes. Smols followed with the tray of warm ginger cinnamon goodness. Tony gave up his chair for Mama J, and Joey and G-Man scooted over to make room for the girls.

"Were we interrupting something? You're all gathered around in one place." Mama J asked. Maybe they shouldn't have just dropped in like this. Or maybe God, in his infinite wisdom, sent them over at this exact time.

"Nah," G-Man leaned back and relaxed his arm on the top of the divan, the picture of nonchalance. "We were just hashing over the day."

"Oh, well, maybe it was good timing. You were probably ready for a little snack." Mama J pointed to the cookie cutouts—reindeer, snowmen, snowflakes iced with dots of confetti sugar. She glanced at the beer cans and nodded to Irene, who held out a jug of milk.

"We thought you'd like some of this to go with the cookies." Ignacia's smile was the epitome of naivety.

Slingshot jumped up, went to the kitchen and brought back a stack of paper cups.

"How is everything, Mama J?" Joey held a cookie to his mouth, then, seeing Rosie's pleading eyes, broke off a piece and gave it to her.

"We're doing well. I wanted to let you know that Sammy Jerard, the detective and Ignacia, who used to be an investigator are working hard at finding your brother."

Joey raised his eyebrows and stopped mid-chew.

"They have a few leads, but no solution yet."

Joey's face fell.

"Don't be discouraged. Our God knows where he is. He won't let you down." Mama J wrapped her fingers around the cross hanging from her neck.

"There is no creature that is hidden from His sight. That's in the Bible—Hebrews 4:13." Irene said, her tone gentle.

"Woah, does that mean that He sees us? Like all the time?" Squirt's shoulders tensed and he scanned the room, his eyes involuntarily landing on the hill in the middle of the coffee table.

Joey gave him the *look*. He had to agree, however that if that was true, they could be in some major trouble. That is, if there really was a God.

Mama J didn't miss the interchange. "We'll just pray to our Lady, the undoer of knots. When there's something all muddled up like a tangled mess of yarn, she's got her way of straightening things out."

"Anyway," Agnes glanced at Mama J, "We wanted to ask you for help."

Joey squirmed in his seat. "What'd you have in mind?" What could they possibly want? Did they know their skills and need them to procure something for them?

"I saw how much you liked the kids at Hope House." Agnes looked at Irene who continued.

"As you know, it'll soon be Christmas." Joey's mind was racing. Did they want them to give them a bunch of presents? Cut down a tree? What?

"And they are going to dress up and perform the Nativity. We were wondering if you might help us out with that."

Joey reached way back in his Catholic upbringing trying to piece this together. Christmas. Nativity. Santa. No, they didn't allow no Santas. Jesus. Must be the baby story.

"What would we need to do?"

"Some of the kids need help with their costumes." Irene reached for a cookie.

"And we need someone to work the lights and draw the curtains." Agnes looked each in the eye.

The tortoise crawled out from under Smols' chair and looked up at him. Smols laughed and went to the kitchen for some lettuce. "You wouldn't need a Santa, would you?"

Mama J put her finger to her lips in thought. "I guess I could ask Brother Ben if that would be okay. I mean, we don't want to take away from the baby Jesus. Anyway, it will be held at St. Michael's the week before Christmas, and if you could help, we'd be ever so grateful."

"I think we could make it, right, boys?" They nodded.

———

AFTER THEY HAD PLACED their headlamps on their heads, Tim followed Sammy and Ignacia down the cellar steps.

"This wasn't exactly the date I had envisioned," Sammy said. "I was thinking more of a candlelight dinner, soft music, great conversation."

"True. All I was thinking about was spending time with you. So, in my mind, this little adventure is as good as a date." Tim smiled and put his arm around her waist.

Ignacia said, "Don't forget what brought us down here. Tim, we heard a loud bang when we were in the basement, and it sounded as if it came from the other side of the wall."

Tim scanned the room. "There's a lot in here, but I don't see anything that would have fallen or caused a sound."

"Could it have been the steel door? Maybe someone had been down here and dropped it shut." Sammy placed her finger on her lip. "What if they come back?"

"It's possible. But let's look on the bright side. If they did, we could ask them about this place. They might know if there's a connection." Tim shrugged. "Nothing is out of place—I mean, it's not like anything was knocked over."

Ignacia paced the perimeter of the walls. Turned out the cellar wasn't nearly as large as their basement. But that didn't exclude the possibility of the walls adjoining and there being a door on this side leading to the basement. One could always hope.

An 1800s large wheel bicycle lay against one wall and a wringer washer beside it. Several dry racks were folded up, and a metal tub held round balls of some sort. Tim picked one up. It fit in his hand.

"These are heavy. Made of iron. They must be cannonballs. Hmmm. I guess this is sort of a museum."

"There's just as much or more junk in here as in the basement." Sammy sighed.

Tim squatted and examined the floor, where men's footprints were impressed in the dirt floor. "Sammy, bring me the plaster kit. I want to take a cast of this footprint."

He opened the kit and withdrew a plastic tub with dry

plaster powder, a stir stick, and bottle of water. He mixed them together and slowly poured the mixture into the print.

"I need to wait ten minutes while it sets."

He sat on a plastic tub, the black sides worn. As he did, the brittle top split in two.

"Oh, wasn't expecting that." He caught his balance and Sammy took his hands and pulled him up.

"Looks like some old magazines. Life, National Geographic."

"Don't get sidetracked with that, Tim. I know you—you'd spend the whole evening finding out interesting facts that have absolutely nothing to do with our goal."

"Sammy, you know me well." Tim smiled. "But maybe when this is over, I could take them back to the office and peruse them. Do you think anyone would miss them?"

"Probably not. Who's to say they even know what's down here. Whoever *they are*."

Tim checked the cast and carefully lifted it into a flat cardboard box.

Ignacia headed to the back wall. "Don't worry about anything except this wall since it would be the one connecting the two." Crates were stacked two deep clear across the wall. She assembly-lined sliding crates to Sammy and on to Tim, who started a new row on the left wall. Dust from the crates covered the front of Ignacia's habit. She shrugged. Sometimes you just had to get down deep and dirty.

Along the back wall was a sturdy set of metal shelves filled with more treasures. A butter churn. Old hand-carved duck decoys. A vintage kerosene lamp, which even held a bit of kerosene. Once they unloaded the shelves, Ignacia walked to the end of the shelf. There was a three-foot gap between it and the left wall. Why hadn't they gone there first? The wall held an old quilt tacked to the ceiling beam with square iron nails.

Irene's hands shook as she grasped the binding of the quilt. Would she finally find what they'd been looking for?

"Do it, Ignacia. Don't hold us in suspense," Sammy put her hand on Ignacia's shoulder. "Bring the light over here, Tim."

He positioned it for optimal vision, and Ignacia slid the faded patchwork quilt to the side. And there it was. A three-by-three-foot door held by the same worn brass hinges as in the basement.

21

WHILE MOST OTHER houses in the neighborhood were decked with wreaths, garlands, lights—some houses with thousands of them, Big Red's abode was dark and gloomy. What was there to like about Christmas, anyway? Life had not treated him good, and he wasn't about to return anything positive to life.

His assault rifle lay in a vice on the table where he meticulously cleaned each part. There was never a time when he wanted to be caught off guard for whatever *situation* arose. He picked up the brass brush, squirted solvent on it, inserted through the breach towards the muzzle and retracted it. His mind ventured to his crypto accounts. They had done quite well, but he wanted more. The accounts, along with the crypto mining had made him what some might call a wealthy man, but he dreamed of buying a far-off private island where he could relax in the sun with his choice of pretty girls. And a jet. And a mansion.

He was interrupted by the sound of the vacuum. Big Red ran a tight ship, and cleanliness was a top priority. Moe ran it through the living room, moving chairs and end tables to clean each spot. Something blocked the vacuum end. Moe bent and looked to see what it was. He picked up a slingshot and frowned, placed it in his hip pocket and continued vacuuming. Big Red took a rag and polished the outside of the gun. Next, he loaded it so it would be ready for whatever came next.

"Do you want me to throw those rags in the laundry?" Big Red nodded and Moe scooped them up and headed downstairs to the washing machine. Big Red watched him go.

"Hey, what's that in your pocket?"

Moe turned and felt, then pulled it out. "I don't know. I guess it's a slingshot. It was under the table."

"Hand it over." Big Red turned it over and squinted. Now why did this look familiar?

It wasn't long before he heard a blood-curdling "Nooooo".

Big Red's expletive overrode Moe's cry and following wail. George's heavy footsteps down the stairs were next. Big Red followed.

"What happened? Why's it dark in here?"

"It's not just dark, Boss. The miners are off."

"What? Who decided today was the day to test my patience! Did you switch off the breaker?"

"No—I already checked that," Moe said. His hands shook uncontrollably.

"And?"

"The wires were cut." Moe ducked as Big Red grabbed him by the shoulders, fire shooting from his eyes.

"I, I, I didn't do it. You know that."

"Great timing. Right in the middle of the biggest chain solve ever."

George cut in. "Someone had to have come in here while we were gone. Maybe the same goons who decorated the house."

Big Red, followed by the other two, ran back upstairs to the chest. He threw off the tablecloth and floral arrangement, which crashed to the floor. He lifted the lid, and their jaws dropped. Empty.

"I'm gonna kill those dirty rats."

TONY ADJUSTED HIS BACKPACK, slid the clasp on the iron gate, and it swung open. The cold weather had turned the grass brown. The last of the red and gold maple leaves had fallen to the ground. They danced along the sidewalk, as a breeze picked them up. It made Tony think of when he was about three. Or was it four? He couldn't remember. But what he did remember, was his older brother Tom taking a rake and making huge piles of leaves that they would run and jump into. It was like landing in a soft wonderland where he would burrow and hide, waiting for his brother to pretend he didn't know where he was. Then he would pop up and giggle, surprising Tom, who would grab him and twirl him around until his head was spinning with the world around him. Good times. If only it had lasted. But maybe, just maybe, he could recreate that relationship with Ivan. Do something good in his life.

Brother Ben answered the door. That man reminded Tony of a big teddy bear—inviting smile, full beard, and a huggable middle. Not that Tony had any plans to hug him. But he could understand why all the kids loved him. There was just something peaceful about him. An air of confidence and peace. Being around him was very different from his usual pals who could be clowns, but each of them had their own sort of angst. Describing them as having peace was not at the top of the list.

"Tony, my friend." Ben clasped Tony's hand and he patted him on the shoulder. "To what do I owe the pleasure?"

"I just thought I'd stop by and check on Ivan. Is that okay?"

"Of course." Ben turned and called for Ivan, who ran to embrace Tony.

"Hey Dude, what's hoppin'?"

Ivan started hopping around him and grinned. "Come on. I want to show you something I made." Ivan pulled Tony's hand and led him to the playroom where there stood a dozen plastic characters, some on the wood floor, and some standing on staggered wooden blocks.

"That looks cool. What are you going to do now?" Tony removed his backpack and set it on the floor. He sat on the floor next to Ivan.

"Brother Ben let me use this nerf dart gun. See what I can do?" Ivan loaded a dart into the plastic gun and shot a character where it fell flat on its face.

"Wow, that's cool. Do you have more darts?"

Ivan dropped a dozen darts in front of Tony.

"Can I see your gun?" Ivan handed it to Tony. "You know you have to play safe with guns, right?" Ivan nodded.

"It's just a toy, you know."

"Yeah, I know, but even toys can hurt people if you're not careful." Tony looked the gun over. It had a barrel with slots for four darts. He loaded all the slots and handed the gun back to Ivan. "Try this."

Tony pulled the trigger and all four shots in succession. His aim was a little off, but several characters fell.

"Oh, my goodness! That's so cool!" Ivan retrieved the darts and reloaded.

"I'm gonna try it again." Before you knew it, he had mastered his skill. There was no hope for the defenseless characters.

Tony smiled. Maybe showing him how to use a toy gun wasn't the best thing to teach him, but who knew if he'd ever need that knowledge. He had come from a war zone, after all.

Tony stood. "I've got to get going. But first, I have something for you." He unzipped his backpack and let Ivan look inside.

Ivan squealed. "A soccer ball! You kept your promise." The grin on his face spread from ear to ear.

As IGNACIA JUMPED up and down, her rosary beads bounced at her side. Finally, the search was over. "I'll crawl through."

"You can't do that. How can you? You're wearing your habit. You'll get caught up in there." Sammy frowned at her.

"And come out filthy. Here, let me do it." Tim removed his coat and handed it to Sammy.

"Be careful. And here, wear this headlamp. I just charged the battery."

Tim smiled at her and took it. After placing it on his forehead, he easily slid the door open. Sammy and Ignacia watched him crawl through the door until just the soles of his shoes showed.

"There's a small tunnel." Tim's voice was muffled. He inched his way forward another five feet. "I've reached the other door."

Ignacia couldn't help jumping up and down. She clasped her hands. Thank you, Jesus. She crossed herself.

"I'm going in." Sammy got to her knees and followed Tim into the basement.

"That's at least one part of the mystery solved." Ignacia squatted to examine the opening. The wood was unpainted. Signs of termites, from the looks of the bits of sawdust and tunneling. The tunnel floor was packed dirt and had signs of entry—besides Sammy and Tim's. Ignacia looked closely at the hinges. There. Several blue and white threads were stuck on the hinges, perhaps a piece of a shirt. Ignacia knew better than to touch them. It could alter the evidence.

"Tim, Sammy, come back. I've found something."

They scooted themselves back, and Ignacia pointed at the threads. "Whoa, now that's worth saving." Tim pulled a sandwich bag from his hip pocket. "Sammy, could you grab the tweezers in my bag?"

He carefully deposited the evidence into the bag.

"Well, friends, I believe we've had a very productive day." Ignacia checked her watch. "If we head to the house now, they should have dinner on the table."

Tim looked at Sammy. "Uh, thanks, Ignacia, but I have a pretty lady I need to take out to dinner." He wrapped his arm around her. Her smile was all the encouragement he needed.

22

WHEN IGNACIA ENTERED the dining room, everyone was seated except Irene, who carried a large, beautiful salad and set it on the table. Edith scrunched up her nose. Mama J, sitting beside her, put her hand gently on hers. Edith's shoulders dropped.

Ignacia's habit was filthy. Cobwebs sticking to it, dirt, and mud. She took a damp rag and brushed the webs and debris off her habit and washed her hands. She was such a mess. Then again, sometimes God's work was messy.

After saying the blessing, they dug into the chicken Alfredo and garlic bread. Ignacia was hangry. She must have forgotten to eat lunch. Unless you called the cookie dough lunch. She had to admit that it had kept her energy up.

"So, Ignacia. Can you update us on what you've found so far?" Mama J asked.

"This whole affair has been a lot. But I'm happy to say we found several things. For one, did you know there's a root cellar behind the house?"

"Really?" Agnes frowned. "How have we missed that?"

"There's a metal trapdoor that was hidden under the grass

and leaves. We found it only because Sammy slipped in the snow. The snow made the metal slippery."

"Did you go in?" Edith asked.

"We did. Those headlamps came in handy. It was cold and dark in there. Makes sense if that's where they kept their vegetables. There were buckets of potatoes, beets, carrots. A dirt floor."

"You had Sammy and Tim with you, right?" Mama J reached for the salad.

"Right. And good thing. Tim brought his bag of forensic stuff with him. But I need to back up. Sammy and I had been in the basement trying to figure out where the entrance was. We'd searched all over, moved boxes and shelves. The one place we hadn't looked was under the stairs. There was a plywood wall attached to part of it, and just as Sammy crawled under and actually found a door, we heard a loud bang. So that's when we went outside to see what it was."

Agnes held a bite midway to her mouth. "Weren't you afraid? I would have been."

"No, I guess we were so focused on solving the mystery. Anyway, the root cellar is several yards smaller than the basement. Tim figured the bang was someone leaving the cellar. It made sense. Maybe they needed potatoes. Probably whoever was cooking dinner at Joey's. We found footprints that might have been theirs. Ignacia took a bite. She needed food.

"Ladies, let's let this poor girl get a bite to eat. She's had a long day."

Irene scooped more salad onto her plate. "But for sure, we want to hear the rest of the story."

Ignacia nodded.

"So, we need to discuss the logistics of the Nativity play. It's coming right up—only two more days. I asked Joey and the crew if they could help out. I'm betting they've never heard the true Christmas story." She crossed herself. "They said they would. So, we need help with costumes, set, lights, curtains. Can you think of anything else?" Mama J looked around.

"Maybe one of them could usher." Agnes held her open hands up, questioning.

"I'm not so sure that would be a good idea. We might scare the audience off," Edith said.

"Okay then, Brother Ben could usher."

Mama J nodded. "We'll have one more rehearsal tomorrow on the school stage to get everything figured out."

Agnes clapped her hands. "This is going to be so fun!"

Ignacia finished her last bite. "That was delicious. Thanks to Irene and Edith. So, here's what we found. There *was* a door from the cellar. Tim crawled through. And I found a few threads stuck to the door hinge. Tim took those back to the lab as well. I would guess they were from whoever shot Michael."

"That's right," Agnes leaned in. "Because remember, Michael had on a white button-down shirt. So, the threads couldn't have been his."

SNOW THAT HAD FALLEN the night before glistened like diamonds covering the local park. It was the perfect day for snowmen and sleds. Brother Ben had rounded up the kiddos into the van—dressed in boots, warm clothing, hats and gloves. He found a spot and parked. Their excitement bounced from the van walls to the ceiling, and beyond. It occurred to Ben that the children had experienced snow before, but perhaps because of the war hadn't been able to have fun in it. He smiled. It was the small joys in life.

"Ivan, grab the snow shovel. Olena, do you have the carrots and buttons? Liliya, bring the sled. I'll keep the hot cocoa in the van for later. Everyone jump out."

The clear blue skies allowed the sun to shine brightly on the snow. It was cold enough to make Ben glad for his bushy beard. It added a small amount of warmth. He adjusted the soft knit scarf Mama J had made for him which he wore over his black cassock.

The park was extensive. It had a small hill, great for sledding, with tall pines and a circle of trees and bushes that created a semi-enclosed space. He didn't like that it was located beside a busy road, but he'd monitor the kids. They were his greatest joy. He didn't want anything to happen to them while in his care. *And Lord, please take care of their parents.*

Liliya helped her brother Bohdan onto the sled and pulled him. The others traipsed ahead a few yards and picked up snow and threw it into the air, watching it fall to the ground.

Across the field, he noticed two men having the time of their lives—just the two of them. It was like they were little kids again, laughing and playing.

"Brother Ben, come on. Help us build a snowman." Olena tugged on his arm. Her words became steam passing from her mouth. Ivan had already shoveled snow into a pile and began rolling a ball.

"Here, Ivan. Let me take over. I'm taller and can do it better." Taras took over when the ball reached Ivan's waist. The snow packed well, and it was deep enough to pack balls for a large snowman. Mykita started another ball for the middle, while Olena worked on the head.

"We need sticks for arms," Mykita said.

Ivan's face wore a frown, and his arms were crossed as he watched Taras take over.

"I can find some."

He tried to run, but the snow was too deep, and he fell. He didn't let that stop him, however, and stood and brushed himself off. He turned and waved at Brother Ben and headed to the nearby trees. Ben continued to watch him as he crossed the field. Out of the corner of his eye, Brother Ben saw a red vehicle pull over to the side of the road.

When Ivan got closer to the trees, he was distracted by the two men who were a short distance away. They had rolled five large snowballs and lined them up. On top of them, they had placed empty cans. The taller man wore a black sweatshirt with the hood covering his head, making it hard to see his face. The other wore his ball cap backwards with blonde bangs hanging in his eyes. He wore a heavy black coat, but not so much as to hinder him from taking his slingshot, placing a stone in it and shooting a can right off the top a snowball.

Ivan realized who it was and hollered at them. "Hey." Ivan waved his mittened hand and started towards them. Tony saw him coming and stayed Slingshot's arm before he shot again.

"Ivan buddy, great to see you." Tony patted him on his head.

"We're building snowmen. I was looking for sticks for arms. And then I saw you." Ivan turned to Slingshot. "That was neat, what you did. Could I try it?"

Slingshot shrugged his shoulders. He had been about this kid's age when his dad had first taught him to use one. "This is how you hold it."

Ivan's hand was small for the size slingshot it was, but he held it tight. "Now, take something small, like a marble, or a stone, and pinch it in this pouch. I'm using marbles."

David demonstrated and handed the device to Ivan. He placed the marble in the pouch, pulled back and let it loose. It went a couple of yards and fell.

"That was cool!" He looked at David for approval.

Brother Ben plodded up beside them and smiled. "Hello friends. He held out his hand. Looks like you're enjoying the snow as well."

"I got to shoot it. Did you see?" Ivan touched Ben's arm.

"I did. It looks like you had fun. We'd better head back to the others. Did you find some arms for the snowman?"

"Not yet. Could you help me?" Brother Ben nodded.

They found several sticks that looked like they might work and sludged back to the others.

"What does Ivan see in that Tony guy? He seems like trouble to me." Taras spoke to Liliya. She frowned and nodded her head towards Ivan, who overheard them. Ivan threw the sticks down, ran to the van and sat down. He put his hands on top of his lowered head.

23

BIG RED PULLED his rig up a few yards. "That might be our guy."

"Which one?" George swiveled in the front seat.

"He's got a slingshot. How many people do you see in D.C. with a slingshot? That has to be him." He held binoculars to his eyes and watched him shoot, the projectile propelling a can into the air.

"He's good." George said. "I'm not sure I could do that. But I can see where it could be quite useful."

"Who's that little kid? It looks like they know each other." He watched a while longer. "I'm in no hurry. We'll just sit and observe. Wait to see which car he drives and follow him."

BACK IN THE LAB, Sammy and Tim were examining the evidence found on the hinge.

"Take a look at this, Sammy." Tim moved away from the microscope.

"This has to be from someone's shirt. There's enough here to see that it was cotton thread, woven into some type of design.

Four blue threads with whites crossing them. My guess is a plaid."

"That helps, I guess." Tim looked through the microscope again. "There's a hair, looks blonde. Now that's something we could go with. That will give us a DNA sample." He looked up, satisfied.

"What about the plaster mold of the footprint? Did you examine that yet?"

Tim went to a drawer and pulled it out, still in the cardboard box. He placed it on the table and then brought Michael Rotoni's boots. He gently pulled out the casting of a left boot and examined the tread. Then compared it to the left boot. He looked up at Sammy.

"Same. So that answers that question. I have another question, though. What type of gun was used to kill Michael?"

Tim shrugged. "We never found a bullet. It was weird."

"Ignacia and I examined the whole room. I would guess a bullet would have lodged in the stone wall behind him, if not in his chest." She frowned and held a knuckle to her chin.

"That would certainly make sense. I'd have to say that is still a mystery."

Sammy texted Ignacia and asked her to look once more in the basement to see if there was any sign of a bullet. And, by the way, the threads were blue and white and appear to have been from a blue flannel shirt. Any ideas?

BERNARDO SLID out of his jeep carrying a large plastic bag filled with presents. He went to the door, knocked tap-tap, tap-tap-tap and opened the door. Amelia came running.

"Daddy!" She wrapped her arms around his legs. "Are those

for me?" She smiled and blinked her long eyelashes. Could his daughter be any cuter than that?

"Some are. There may be some from Santa in there too." Bernardo winked.

"Santa doesn't come until Christmas eve. You know that! And some for Mom? You have to have something for Mom. She would be so happy."

He hoped she'd be happy. But he knew that nothing was going to really make her happy until their daughter was healthy.

Bernardo nodded and lay the bag down next to the small artificial tree. Amelia plugged in the lights. "Mom only lets me turn them on sometimes. She says they take too much 'lectricity."

Bernardo was glad that he would soon be able to fix that. Their take from the heist would net a huge profit once they figured out where to pawn the gold bars.

Marie walked out of the bathroom, twisting a tie around her frizzy hair. She gave Bernardo a quick hug and kissed his cheek.

"I was just getting ready to take a pizza out of the oven. Can you stay?"

Amelia glanced his way.

Bernardo nodded. "And when did you say the small fry's appointment was?"

"Today. At 2:00. You didn't forget, did you?" She frowned.

"I thought so, but I wasn't sure. I don't want to miss it. This is about her pre-op, right?"

He glanced at Amelia as she placed the packages neatly under the tree. He was feeling positive about seeing her again next Christmas. Until they received the payload, he wasn't sure they could afford surgery. But now? Things were looking pretty good.

Marie pulled on mitts and slid the pizza out of the oven. She took a pizza roller out of the drawer and cut the pizza into slices.

Bernardo pulled plates from the shelf and set them on the table, two large and one plastic with a picture of Cinderella.

———

"Marie, Bernardo, I'm Dr. Halahan." He shook their hands. "I'll be Amelia's surgeon. I'd like to go over what happens next."

They nodded. Marie stuck her hands under her thighs and leaned in. Bernardo could hear his heart thudding in his chest. Thoughts of the jail time causing him to miss a full two years of his little girl. Two years of firsts he could never regain.

"Amelia has TOF, Tetralogy of Fallot with Pulmonary Atresia." Dr. Halahan paused.

Marie looked at Bernardo. "That's a long name for congenital heart defect. It's very common in infants and children. Her heart is not functioning correctly, not pumping blood the way it's supposed to. The pathway from her heart to her lungs is too narrow—almost completely blocked—so she isn't getting enough oxygen."

"That's why she's been so tired all the time, isn't it," Marie said.

Dr. Halahan nodded. "What I'm going to say next may cause you angst, but you need to know that my team and I have done thousands of these surgeries successfully. And I expect the same outcome with your precious daughter."

Bernardo's heart rate increased. He tried to slow his breathing, but hearing this news? It definitely wasn't easy.

"First, we'll completely anesthetize her. Then we'll open her chest, place her on a heart-lung machine, widen the outflow tract, and close the hole between the chambers of her heart. I'll patch the ventricular septal defect, reconstruct the pulmonary artery, and ensure blood can flow freely to her lungs."

Too many big words. He wanted to get to the point. "How long will she be in surgery?" Bernardo asked.

"Five to six hours. It's a delicate procedure. We'll keep you posted throughout."

Marie let out a sigh, and a tear slipped down her cheek.

"I realize it's hard not to worry. But surgery is her best option. Without it, there's no telling how long she'll live. With it, she should live a normal, active life."

Marie nodded and leaned into Bernardo's shoulder. He put his arm around her and kissed the top of her head.

BIG RED LAID the binoculars on the console between his seat and George's.

"It looks like they're finally wrapping things up. Wonder what the big guy is telling our *friends*."

"Hard to say, but they've got some kind of connection for sure."

It wasn't long before everyone was loaded and they pulled out.

Big Red pushed start and his red beast came to life. He watched the priest, or the brother, whatever you called that guy in the black costume, get into the van and pull out onto the road. Red waited until he saw that evil son of a viper with the slingshot get into a white Toyota pickup and pull out.

He wanted to give just the right amount of space to not be noticed. Not that it was easy to ignore a large red vehicle. He followed them west on Taylor Street along the edge of the park and turned left on 13th Street. A stoplight on the corner of Taylor stopped Big Red after the pickup and the van already slid through. Big Red cursed and pounded the steering wheel. His eyes scanned the cross street. No cops, and he gunned through the red light.

"What's your plan? Are we gonna snag them?" George pulled out a lighter and lit a cigarette.

"No. I just want to see where they land and come back later."

He was glad to have a high-seated vehicle to see over the cars. He caught up and watched as both vehicles turned left onto Otis and pulled up to an iron gated yard. George snapped a photo of the place as they drove by.

"I think that's all we need to know for now." Big Red rolled down the window and spat before he roared off.

24

MAMA J WALKED through the convent carrying a list and giving orders. The kitchen counters were full of five apple and lemon meringue pies, five dozen decorated Christmas cookies, a large pan of fresh cinnamon rolls, two dozen lemon tarts and two trays of savory appetizers. Edith filled a bag with fixings for hot apple cider, a ladle and cups.

"I think this will be enough for refreshments after the Nativity. Go ahead and load them into the van." Mama J watched them leave and turned to the living room.

Ignacia folded each of the costumes, labeled individual bags, as Irene checked names off their list. "Vova - sheep, Taras and Liliya - Wisemen, Olena - shepherd, Mykita is an angel, Iryna - Mary, Bohdan - Joseph, Ivan - Gabriel. That should be good. At least that's the way I have it on the program. I'm pretty sure they each know their parts."

"This is going to be so much fun! I can't wait." Ignacia grinned.

Mama J smiled and nodded to the ceiling. She was sure God was watching and looking out for them. This wasn't just about a cute little play. This was about the birth of the Savior. And she hoped it would be a defining moment for their little charges.

With everything loaded, they headed to the church auditorium where they would meet Ben, the kids and their friendly neighbors who agreed to help.

BROTHER BEN STOOD at the end of the dinner table commanding attention. They had just finished the day with homemade mac and cheese, Little Cuties, garlic bread and topped the meal off with a dish of vanilla ice cream with caramel topping and sprinkles. They had eaten early since they had to be at the church by five to get ready for their play.

He fixed his eyes on each child, saying a silent prayer over each. His one Christmas wish was that the war would be over, and they could be re-united with their parents. He would desperately miss them but knew that whatever time he had left with them was in God's time.

"Let's talk through what to expect tonight. First, there will be a lot of people coming to watch you. So don't be surprised."

"I'll be scared," Mykita said. She pulled on one of her braids.

"You don't need to be scared, silly. You're just an angel. You don't have to say anything." Olena put her arm around her.

"The nuns will fix your hair and make-up," Brother Ben continued.

"Ewwww... make-up." Bohdan made a face.

"It'll just be a little bit so the audience can see you better. Your costumes are in bags and labeled, so there shouldn't be any confusion about what to wear. After it's over, there will be refreshments and a surprise."

"A surprise?" Iryna clapped her hands, her eyes sparkled and she had a huge grin spreading across her face.

Ben said, "We won't have time to mess around. As soon as we arrive, Tony and the rest will be there to help get your costumes on."

"Tony." Taras said under his breath. He scrunched up his nose and shook his head.

"What's with you?" Ivan said. "I like him."

"I think he's a jerk, and you should stay away from him."

Ivan pushed his chair over and ran out of the room.

Brother Ben watched him go. This wasn't the first time Ivan had gotten mad and hid. He'd give him some time and look for him in a bit.

"All right, take your plates to the kitchen, go brush your teeth. If your clothes are wet or muddy from the snow, change them. Be quick about it. Someone help Vova. Mikyta?" She nodded, took his plate with hers and held his hand.

***

"Where's Bernardo?" Joey looked around.

"He said he was going to stay in the audience. He wanted to sit with his wife and daughter. She's been pretty sick." Smols slid his legs through his Santa pants and pulled up the suspenders.

"The kids should be here any minute. I'm surprised we got to the church before they did." David snapped the pouch on his slingshot.

"Put that thing away. Act like an adult. We got to be good examples to those little kids." Joey's gold teeth glinted under the show lights, which Slingshot was testing.

G-Man held a box of clip-on mics. "Tony, help me test the batteries."

Mama J entered followed by the rest of the sisters. "Oh good, you're already getting things in order. Thank you. You all are sure life savers."

Edith and Irene carried trays of cookies past the men. Smols reached for one, and Edith held the tray back. "Just wait. There are plenty. You'll get some after the show."

Slingshot shone a spotlight on the cookies as they were carried across the stage.

"Hey ladies, don't you ever get to wear pants or something else? It must be boring wearing those dress thingy's all the time." Irene shook her head and rolled her eyes.

Mama J stood back and checked the set. The stable was the same one that had been used for years. Four posts, a thatched roof, a silver star attached to the peak. The manger sat inside with a little straw thrown in. She walked to the back of the stage and checked her props list—staff for the shepherd, a crown for the Wisemen, the baby and blanket, and the chest for the Wisemen. Oh, and the balloon for under Mary's costume and the stick donkey. She looked up at the excited sound of little voices.

"You're here. Just in time. Come in and sit in a semi-circle on the floor. Squirt, could you hand each child their costumes? The bags are labeled."

Ignacia set up the podium where she would read the scriptures. Squirt and the other men each picked a child and began helping them with their costumes.

"Vova, let's get you into this sheep costume." Squirt unzipped the full-length zipper and helped him place his feet into the legs. Vova held his arms out for the sleeves. Vova put the headpiece on himself and attached the Velcro under his chin.

"Now don't you look cute. You coulda weared that for Halloween." Vova got on all fours and baa-ed. Squirt smiled. He'd never had a costume before. Never went out for Halloween. Was never in a play. And why was there a sheep in a Jesus story, anyway?

Smols helped Bohdan with his costume. "I think you put this blue thing on first."

"Yeah, that's right. It's my tunic. And then the jacket next." He slipped his arm through. "Why are you wearing a Santa suit?"

Smols looked down. "Is that what this is?"

"Don't you know anything?"

Smols laughed. "I thought Santa was in the play."

"Santa's not in the play. You should know that." Bohdan circled his index finger near his temple, crazy.

Smols pursed his lips. He *should* know that. And he did, didn't he? He tried to remember if he had ever seen this story before.

"And what's in that big bag?" Bohdan asked as he started to grab it.

"Just never you mind. That belongs to Santa."

Seeing that everyone was in costume, Ignacia reminded the actors where they should stand and when to come on stage. She directed Joey to open and shut the curtains and gave him and the others a copy of the script. Meanwhile, the kids started chasing each other. Mykita climbed onto a set box, spread her wings and jumped, which knocked her wire halo crooked. Ignacia threw her hands on her head.

"Children. Freeze." They stood stock still. "Come stand in a line and let me take one last look at you before you go backstage. People are beginning to come in." She counted heads and frowned. We're short one."

Brother Ben leaned against the stage and counted. "Where's Ivan?"

They all looked around. "Has anyone seen him?" Mikyta shrugged. Taras shook his head. Olena frowned. Ben hopped onstage. "I'll check in the back."

Tony jumped in. "Ivan is missing? I'll check the bathroom."

Edith and Irene entered. "Have you seen Ivan?"

"He wasn't in the kitchen." Edith threw her hands up.

Mama J's stomach tightened. She prayed, "St. Anthony, help us find him." Then, "And if you can't, ask Jesus to help."

25

MAMA J SCANNED THE AUDIENCE. "The auditorium is filling quickly."

The room buzzed with happy laughter, and anticipation. Sammy and Tim were seated a few rows from the front. Mama J watched a couple walk down the aisle, each holding hands with a blonde-headed girl wearing a fancy red Christmas dress and white stockings, who tugged on them, eager to see the show.

She wished the Hope House kids' parents could be here as well to watch their children perform. Perhaps someone would video the performance and if and when the day came, she could share it.

After the hubbub of everyone searching for Ivan, and not finding him, Ignacia, hands wringing, asked Joey to close the curtains. She called everyone onto the stage.

Ignacia needed to make a quick decision. "I hate to do this, but we're going to have to start without him. I'll just skip his part."

"That little rat is always getting mad and running away." Taras rolled his eyes. "He probably planned to ruin the program."

Brother Ben put his hand on Taras's shoulder and gave him the *look*.

"I'm going to run home and see if he's there. I'll call Mama J and let her know. I'm sure it'll be okay. You kids do your best. Remember, we're representing Jesus." He winked.

———

GEORGE DROVE Big Red's rig and slowed in front of the iron-fenced yard with a sign that said Hope House.

"Hope—well, we'll see. I hope that slingshot guy is still here," Red said.

All the lights were off. Fudge. He rolled down the window and took a closer look.

"What's that sound?" George said.

Moe rolled his window down. "Sounds like crying."

This might be the opportunity Red needed. George cut the engine and Red slid out, his boots crunching the snow. Squinting, he cocked his head to listen. Where was the crying coming from?

He slid the gate latch open and stepped into the yard. There he was. A little boy sitting on the front steps, sniffling. His arms were wrapped around his chest, a vain attempt to keep from shivering.

Big Red towered over the boy, wool hat snug on his head. "Hey." He squatted down at eye level. The boy looked up. "What's your name?"

"Ivan."

"What are you doing out here in the cold?"

"Nothin'. They left without me." Ivan wiped his nose with the back of his hand.

"Now, that wasn't a very nice thing to do, was it? Locked you out, did they? So, nobody's home?"

Ivan shook his head.

"Would you like me to take you to them? I've got some time. And you could ride in my fancy red G-Wagon."

Ivan looked at the man, then through the fence to his rig. "Who are you?"

"My name's Big Red." He put his hand out to shake. Ivan reluctantly took it.

"Who else is gonna be there?"

"Tony and Slingshot and some of their friends."

Red narrowed his eyes. Yeah, his friends who stole from him. His Majesty of the Mini-Mob would be sorry they ever thought about messing with him.

Red pulled Ivan to his feet. "Come on. Tell me where you need to go and I'll swing by."

Ivan followed him to his rig, where Big Red opened the back door and helped him up.

"It's a big church. I think it's pretty close." Ivan put on his seatbelt and snapped it in place. The leather seats were cold, and he shivered.

Knowing where churches were didn't come naturally for Red. They weren't exactly something he paid attention to when driving around.

"George, get a location." He opened Maps on his phone and pulled up a church. He showed Ivan the photo. "Is this it?"

Ivan nodded. "Everyone's going to be mad at me. I'm supposed to be the angel Gabriel, and now I'm late, and they're not going to let me in the play." Ivan's shoulders tensed. He gripped the handle as George sped up.

There was nowhere to park, so George let Red and Ivan out in front of the church.

"Jump out. Let's hurry," Red said, then turned to George. "I'll let you know when I'm ready to be picked up."

Red watched them drive off and found a side door that

opened into a hall leading to the empty foyer. The lights were dimmed. Red's eyes made a quick search where he found stairs partitioned by a red velvet cord, leading to the balcony. He whispered, "Let's go up here. No one will see you, but you can watch."

———

MAMA J OPENED HER TEXT. Brother Ben saw no sign of Ivan. She shook her head. Ben had just shown up, and was standing at the doorway where he could usher people in. The auditorium was packed, and the clock showed one minute to showtime. She blew out a breath and looked up, reminding God that he was in charge. About that—God being in charge? She knew this to be true. But sometimes, knowing and feeling it were two different things.

Ignacia walked to the middle of the stage in front of the closed blue velvet curtains. The audience quieted like the tide— a gentle incoming wave.

"We'd like to welcome everyone here tonight. Our children have worked hard on this, and I think you'll agree that this is a production that would make anyone proud. With that, let's begin."

G-Man started soft, instrumental music. Joey pulled the cord to open the curtains, where Mary stood spotlighted in the middle of the stage. Ignacia walked to the podium where her open Bible sat.

"God sent the angel to Mary in Nazareth and told her..."

The angel moved to the middle of the stage next to Mary and said, "You're gonna have a baby."

"Huh? I'm not even married. How can that be?"

"Well, God says you're gonna have a baby and you're going to name him Jesus."

"Well, okay then." Mary shrugged and they walked offstage.

"HEY, no fair. Mykita took my place. That was supposed to be me!" Ivan teared up. Big Red frowned and shushed him.

"IN THOSE DAYS, Caesar Augustus issued a decree that a census should be taken of the entire Roman world."

Ignacia glanced stage right, where Squirt gave Mary and Joseph stick donkeys and prodded them onstage.

Mary, who walked awkwardly with a balloon under her tunic, straddled the donkey beside Joseph.

Ignacia read, "Since there were so many people in Bethlehem for the census, there was no room for them to stay the night."

"Where are we going to stay, Joseph? I think this baby's about to come out."

"We'll find a place. Don't worry. Hey mister, do you have anywhere for us to stay? My wife's having a baby."

"The time came for the baby to be born, and she gave birth to a son. She wrapped him in cloths, and placed him in a manger."

Ignacia continued, "There were shepherds in the field nearby keeping watch over their flocks by night."

From stage left, Smols sent out the shepherd and sheep on all fours. "Baa, baa."

He whispered, "Okay, angel, your turn."

She ran up to them and said, "Hey guys, there's a baby. You have to go see him. He's good news." She pointed to the manger and they followed her finger.

"So, they hurried off and found Mary and Joseph, and the baby, lying in the manger."

The shepherd said, "He's so tiny. I'm going to go tell everyone about him."

Vova the little lamb, baa-ed.

BIG RED FIDGETED in his seat. When was this going to be over? He was waiting for just the right time. He had to do this without complications. There was only one thing on his mind, and that was confronting Slingshot and getting the gold back.

WHILE IGNACIA READ, the angel came in carrying a star attached to a large pole.

"And the wise men saw a bright star in the east and told King Herod...

Taras straightened his turban. "We heard the King of the Jews was born. We saw his star and want to worship him." He walked offstage.

"And Herod sent them to go find the baby and let him know where he was. They followed the star that went in front of them and stopped where the baby lay. When they found the baby, the bowed down and offered him gold."

TARAS RETURNED FROM STAGE RIGHT, pulling a closed wooden chest by a rope. He stopped in front of the baby and opened the lid towards the audience. Inside lay gleaming bars of gold.

26

BIG RED'S JAW SLACKENED, his eyes wide and the whites showing. He leaned forward for a better look. He stared as if he just witnessed a miracle which in essence, he had. Now *this* was a piece of luck. Maybe there was a God in heaven.

He now knew what he needed to do. Nothing was going to get in his way. He stood, shoved Ivan from his seat, and grabbed him from behind. Ivan startled and tried to scream. Red clamped his large hand over his mouth and carried him , kicking and struggling, down the stairs.

"Stay still, you little brat," Red whispered, "I'm not playing games. I wouldn't like to see a cute little boy like you end up as collateral damage."

AS THE WISEMAN knelt before the manger, Joey scowled at Squirt. "What are you doing? Why is the gold here?"

"I just thought it would make the scene more real. And besides, we could hide it in plain sight. People won't think it's real." Joey slapped Squirt on the back of his head and looked at Smols. Smols shrugged his shoulders.

. . .

IVAN'S EYES grew as large as the full moon when Red jumped the last step to the foyer. Red jogged down the aisle towards the stage. A baby whimpered. His dad glanced at his mom, who pulled him to her shoulder and covered him with a blanket. An eerie silence stilled the room, the hum of the heater the only sound.

Ivan squirmed and gave a muffled scream as Big Red drug him onstage and faced the cast. The Wisemen and angel froze, their eyes wide in fear.

Ivan licked Red's hand, hoping to get away. Red frowned and shivered, then set Ivan down. He wrapped his fingers around Ivan's neck, pulled a revolver from his back and held it to Ivan's head. A communal gasp came from the audience, and Olena screamed.

Mama J cast a look skyward. "God, this is not the answer I expected to my prayer. What do you have in mind?" She crossed herself. The babe in Mary's arms and the serene scene of worship became fragile and out of place in contrast.

Taras white-knuckled the edge of the gold chest and pulled it off-stage where Bernardo closed the lid and hid it in the costume closet behind a set piece.

BERNARDO'S JAW DROPPED. Amelia turned to him, her wide eyes beginning to tear up. No way was he going to sit here and watch things play out. Sitting in the first three seats of the next to the last row couldn't have been a better choice. He grabbed Amelia by one hand and Marie by the other and ran the few steps out the door.

"Marie, run. Take Amelia and drive home. Be careful. I need to stay here."

Tears formed in Marie's eyes. Bernardo gave her a quick hug. "Go! Now!" He watched them speed off in the car, then ran to the back of the stage.

SMOLS HELD a finger to his lips and dug in his bag.

"G-Man, quick, help me hand these out." Smols emptied his Santa bag onto the stage. What were to have been gifts for the kids scattered the floor.

"What in the name of all that's holy?" Ignacia hastened to herd the kids who were onstage behind the rear curtain. Seeing the pile of guns, she nodded to Smols and whispered, "Keep quiet. Everyone take one and be ready to use it. It looks like we have a war on our hands."

"I'm scared." Vova trembled, and tears poured down his cheeks.

"Shhhh, Vova." Ignacia put her hand on Edith's shoulder. "Edith, take him out the back to a safe spot."

Edith, glad to have an excuse to leave, picked him up, his lamb legs dangling, and carried him out.

Taras stood over the guns, trying to decide which Nerf gun to take. There were all sizes and capabilities. Some were one-shots —some had cartridges that held ten darts complete with a scope.

"Hurry and decide!"

He settled on the largest one, held it to his eye and swung it around.

Smols took Taras by the shoulders and positioned him behind the rear curtain. "Keep an eye out. Don't shoot until I tell you."

Irene reached for a Super Soaker and positioned herself next to Taras.

. . .

"Give me the gold and no one gets hurt." Ivan stood paralyzed, Red's arm wrapped around his neck, squeezing it tight—the cold metal of the gun above his ear.

Tim reached for his phone, then changed his mind. His hand drifted to Sammy's and entwined his fingers in hers.

Red turned towards the audience where he slowly and pointedly looked at each person.

"No one leaves. Understood?"

Joey's eyes narrowed. This was not going to happen on his watch. Now was his chance to get even with this bargain-bin kingpin. Cleaning out his wealth was great, but that wasn't going to be enough. Big Red was going down. Maybe Squirt putting the gold in the chest was the best thing that could have happened. It drew Big Red here. Endangering the kid, however, wasn't cool.

Tim pulled Sammy to the floor. "Stay down." His whisper seemed loud.

Brother Ben, watching from the rear of the auditorium, turned on the house lights and ran through the foyer and out the front door. He scooted down the side of the building and entered the backstage. Locking eyes with Mama J, he turned and peered through the curtains. The audience was visibly frightened. But more than that, Ben felt he had to protect the children and save Ivan at all cost.

On either side of the foyer, two men appeared. Their figures were imposing, standing legs spread and arms crossed. This was not looking good. They had to be part of the kidnapper's gang.

Agnes grabbed a paintball gun, looked it over and nodded her head confidently.

Mama J started for a gun and changed her mind. She'd use the old two-fingers under the apron trick instead.

"YOU THINK you can just hide behind the curtains? That ain't gonna work."

Red glanced behind him, drug Ivan with one hand gripping him by the ear and with the other, pointed the gun at the audience. Taking a few steps backwards, he tripped over the manger and landed inside, his legs dangling over the edge. His gun went off and shot a stage light. Glass shattered and rained down on the stage. Ivan scrambled stage left and ran to Brother Ben, grabbing hold of both legs. Ben wrapped his arms tightly around him.

THE SISTERS and kids were positioned at each of the three curtain openings, holding their guns poised, waiting for Joey's signal.

MEANWHILE, Moe and George sprinted down the aisles and hopped onto the stage.

"NOW!" Joey gave the signal.

Irene was the first to shoot. She aimed the Super Soaker first towards Big Red, spraying him enough to disarm him. She swerved the gun and blasted Moe and George. From the other direction, Taras blasted his Elite 2.0 Commander RD-6 at Moe from behind, hitting with the full ten darts.

Moe turned towards the curtain to go after the shooter. Olena ran from behind the curtain and jumped on George's back, digging her fingernails into his face. Meanwhile, little Bohdan ran in, head down, and barreled into George, knocking him off balance. As he fell, Olena jumped and ran offstage.

Agnes parted the curtains and shot paint balls which splatted on the back of Moe's bald head and then aimed at George. She pulled the trigger, and George jumped as his chest dripped red paint.

MAMA J HAD HAD ENOUGH. She walked boldly onto the stage, her fingers under her apron pointing like a gun, and confronted Big Red. His clothes were drenched and water dripped onto the stage.

"What does your mama think of you being in a gang?" Her eyes travelled up his torso to his wet face—twelve inches higher than her own.

Red was caught off guard. Who did she think she was bringing his mother into the scene? No one had a right to talk about his mom.

"Put your hands up." He held his gun towards the ceiling.

"I'm not going to do that." Mama J stood to her full five feet three and squared her shoulders.

Red said, "I have a gun."

"I see that. I too have a gun. But my better weapon is Jesus." She held her cross up.

Red took two steps back.

Joey watched from behind the curtain. He couldn't let this happen. Jesus or not, he was going in to protect her. He parted the curtains and walked calmly to Big Red.

"Leave her alone. This isn't about her or any of the rest." With Joey's outstretched arm, he moved Mama J out of the way.

Red pursed his lips and nodded his head. So, this was how it was gonna play out.

"I see how this is. You thought you could crash my house and steal my gold. That's not how this is gonna play out."

Joey crossed his arms. "You think we stopped at your gold, fool? We've got all your crypto locked up too. You're just a shadow playing tough in the light."

Red's eyes narrowed. His face turned red as his blood pressure rose. His fingernails dug into his left palm, and with his right hand, he lowered the gun to Joey's chest.

27

THE AUDIENCE LEANED FORWARD, frozen half-way out of their seats. Children leaned into the firm embrace of their parents.

Ignacia whispered to the adults to hustle the kids out of the building. Tony picked up Ivan, who clung to his neck. Smols hoisted Bohdan onto his shoulders and held Iryna's hand, while Squirt led Olena and Mykita to Edith and Agnes, who held the back door open.

In the three-foot soundbox, situated just under the tall ceiling, stood David. After positioning the spotlight on Moe, he drew his slingshot from his rear pocket, positioned a small stone, pulled back the leather pocket and let loose.

In seconds, the stone hit its mark. Moe moaned, fell and grabbed his thigh as blood flowed from the wound. No sooner than Red turned to look, David pulled out another stone and shot George in the butt, where he danced up and down, cried out and threw his hand on the wound.

SAMMY INCHED herself back into her seat, her eyes glued to

David. Her head turned right then left, then right, then left, like a clock pendulum.

Within seconds, David pulled two more stones and shot Red through the stomach and arm, causing him to fall to the floor on his knees.

The audience whooshed a collective breath.

Joey kicked the gun from Red's hand and picked it up. He should shoot him now and be done with that thorn in his side. Then again, he didn't like the thought of ending up within four walled bars for the rest of his life.

Instead, he kicked Red's side and knocked him to his back. Red moaned, and Joey straddled him, placing a heavy boot on each of Red's hands.

"How ya feeling there, Buddy? Looks like this didn't turn out the way you expected now, did it?"

Red closed his eyes in pain.

"Look at me! Where did you bury my brother?"

Red's eyes were half-mast.

Joey picked up his foot and stomped hard on his wrist.

"I asked you a question! Do I need to repeat it?"

"I don't know." Red turned his head.

"Who does know? I'm not stopping till I find out."

"Maybe..." Red's voice trailed off.

Sirens wailed, and Joey turned towards the sound. He stepped down. They could take it from here.

Heads in the audience turned around as Officer Bradley crouched and took measured steps—gun in hand, followed by five other officers.

"Call an ambulance."

Joey glanced around and stepped away.

Slingshot scrambled down the ladder and hopped onto the stage to ascertain the damage. He nodded his head in satisfaction. If only his brother could see him now. Joey gave him a thumbs up.

Officer Bradley leaned against the front of the stage. He scanned the scene—the splintered manger, the water-soaked floor, red paint splattered over the blue curtains. Three injured men.

"Looks like this nice little Nativity play turned into a way different kind of drama."

———

AGNES AND EDITH had picked up Vova and guided the rest of the kids to the room furthest from the auditorium and seated them on the floor.

Edith left and returned with a box of bottled water, which she handed out. Ignacia pulled her braids back and enclosed them in a scarf, which she tied at the top of her head. She needed something to be in order, and this was one thing she had control over.

She began singing Away in a Manger, and the children joined her. It was quiet, calming, and set their minds on the purpose of the evening. She looked at each child, still dressed in costume, and reflected on who they were. Bohdan's headdress was crooked. His eyes vacant, as he mumbled the words. Little Vova sat on Mykita's lap, her arms cradled around him, filling the gap that his parents should have filled.

Ivan leaned on Tony's shoulder. This had been a trauma no little child should have lived through. Bringing the children to Hope House should have been a respite from the war, not an entering into more of the same. The song ended.

"Let's all take a calming breath." Ignacia drew a square in the air, showing them how to inhale and exhale at each turn of the shape.

Brother Ben entered. "Who's ready to go home?"

A room full of hands raised. "Let's go and get some rest. Perhaps Sviatyi Mykolai will have visited while we were gone."

Liliya's eyes sparkled. "That means it's December 19th?" She turned to Iryna and hugged her. "Maybe there will be presents."

Ignacia's heart swelled seeing smiles on their faces and a bit of excitement. And a seed of an idea was born.

TIM PUSHED THE KEY FOB, and his car lights blinked. He held the car door open for Sammy, who slid into the seat. She closed her eyes and let her head fall back on the headrest. He got in and turned to her.

"Are you okay?" He rested his hand on her arm.

She nodded. "I think so. That was intense."

"I know, right? It was supposed to be a little play. A reminder of why we celebrate Christmas." He shook his head in unbelief.

Sammy shifted in her seat, turning to Tim. "But now we have the answer as to who killed Michael."

"We do?" Tim blinked.

"Yes! Don't you see? We never found a bullet. But remember that stone lodged in Michael's head? You wondered about that too because, for sure, it was strange."

"So, you're saying it was a slingshot, which means..."

"David." They both said his name at the same time.

"What do we do now?" Tim entwined his fingers with hers.

"I guess we have to turn him in. We don't really have a choice, do we?" Sammy dipped her head.

"I guess not. But you seem reluctant."

"I am. I guess I shouldn't be, but he seems so nice. A little goofy maybe, but still..."

"You should ask Ignacia since she's been on this case with you."

Sammy nodded. "We still haven't solved what happened to Robbie, Joey's little brother. That's why Ignacia was helping me to begin with."

"It's late now. Let's sleep on it and see what else we can uncover tomorrow." Tim gave her a kiss on the cheek and started the car.

28

"Tony, put on Christmas music. We can't open presents without that final touch." Brother Ben patted Tony's back.

"Sure thing." Tony pulled out his phone and synced it to the Bluetooth speaker. Frosty the Snowman came on, and he hummed along, bringing memories of childhood sing-a-longs when he was a kid.

Ben had set up the common area with all the spare chairs he could find. There needed to be room for the sisters and their friendly neighbors. The room buzzed with excitement. A large Christmas tree stood in front of the picture window, decorated with homemade ornaments—paper chains, folded angels, macaroni pieces glued together spray-painted gold.

Dozens of wrapped gifts sat patiently under the tree waiting for the excited looks and squeals that were to come. The local parish had been generous. Ben wanted this Christmas to be one they would remember—in a good way. He could never erase the trauma of the night, but he would do what he could.

"I sure wish there were something we could do to reunite those kids with their parents," Smols said to Joey.

"But how? Does anyone even know if their parents are still living? Or safe? Or how to reach them, for that matter."

"I'm sure Ben has their contacts."

Ben stood in front of the tree and clasped his hands together. His voice boomed over the hubbub. "Who's ready to open gifts?"

"We are!" Ivan ran and slid on his knees to within inches of the tree. "Come on, everyone." He looked around and waved them over.

"First, we thank God for keeping everyone safe. Especially Ivan."

In a small voice, Ivan said, "It was really scary. At first, I thought Big Red was really nice." Ivan looked down and picked at a piece of fuzz on the carpet. He looked up.

"You were probably mad that we left without you." Ben knelt to make eye contact with Ivan.

Ivan gave a small nod.

"We looked everywhere for you," Taras said.

"And we didn't realize you weren't with us until we were at the auditorium," Olena said. "We didn't mean to leave you."

"Yeah, we like you, Ivan," Vova said in his little voice.

Ivan nodded. "Can we just open presents now?"

Ben smiled and nodded. "Iryna, would you like to help pass them out?"

Iryna stood next to Ben, who took a gift and read the name. Iryna took the flat package to Taras who ripped it open and pulled out a glow in the dark Frisbee. He curled it into his elbow, trying it out without flinging it. He smiled.

"This one is for Bohdan from Bernardo." Bohdan took the rectangular box from Iryna and ripped off the paper. Before he lifted the lid, he glanced at Bernardo, whose lips turned up as he nodded.

He jumped and ran to Bernardo to give him a hug. "It's bunny slippers! Yay! How did you know I wanted these?"

Bernardo chuckled. "Because you told me, silly."

Bohdan held up an index finger. "Wait, I have a gift for you." He retrieved it and handed the small box to him. "Open it."

Inside was a handmade ornament in the shape of an oval with swirls of purples and blues. "I made that for you on the 3-D printer. Brother Ben taught me how."

"It's beautiful. Thank you. You're very talented. Amelia will love this."

It took more than an hour to open all the gifts. Mama J savored every moment. Who would have thought that a bunch of kids from across the ocean, some sisters and ex-cons could have come together for a beautiful celebration? God certainly had his ways and purposes. Now, if He would answer her prayer about finding Robbie. That would be the whole enchilada.

Bernardo sauntered up with two cups of hot apple cider and offered one to Mama J.

She smiled. "Why, thank you. You didn't have to do that."

He shrugged his shoulders. "It's not much." He took a sip and paused. "So, I wanted to apologize for taking your van." He looked at the floor where his foot was worrying the carpet. "I know it caused you a whole lot of trouble."

Mama J put her hand on Bernardo's shoulder and looked him in the eye.

"It did indeed. But, and here's a lesson for you, young man. God is in control of everything. You meant it as a means to an end. But God meant it for good."

"How's that?"

"That van was in pretty rough shape, as I'm sure you know. But because you took it, we were able to receive a brand new one. So essentially, you were who God chose to execute his plan."

Bernardo wasn't sure what to think of that. But he looked up and said, "Thank you, Jesus."

"Thank you, Jesus indeed! How is your daughter?"

"We have surgery scheduled for next week."

"How are you feeling about that?"

Bernardo shrugged his shoulders.

Mama J touched his arm. "I'll pray that God gives you and your wife peace about it. And that Amelia has full healing."

Bernardo turned his head. He couldn't reply with the lump in his throat and he didn't need her to see the tears forming in his eyes.

The kids scattered, playing with their new gifts. Smols and Joey walked over to Mama J. "We were just talking. Is there any possibility of reuniting the kiddos with their parents? They've been away from them for so long."

Mama J frowned. "Funny you should say that. Ignacia had just asked me the same thing. But how would we go about it?"

"Not sure, exactly."

"First we pray, then we see what God's answer will be."

"OFFICER BRADLEY, we have an answer about Michael Rotoni. I'm sure you'd like to hear us out." Tim and Sammy sat in leather office chairs at the police station.

"I would indeed. Tell me what you know."

Sammy crossed her legs. "You know that Ignacia and I thoroughly searched the basement where he was found. We looked both for a clue to what type of gun was used and searched for an entrance point. We knew he and the killer wouldn't have come through the stairs because of the heavy pantry shelf that hid the door."

Tim leaned in and continued, "There was a direct entry to his heart that appeared to be a fatal gunshot wound. The odd thing was, we couldn't find a bullet."

"But," Sammy continued, "when we were at the Nativity and we saw David shoot his slingshot, which nailed Moe, George and Big Red, well, it was clear what happened."

"I have to say, I was impressed. He's pretty good with that thing," Tim said.

Officer Bradley cupped his chin with his hand, and his eyes moved to the ceiling. "So, what you're saying is that I need to bring David in for questioning."

"Yes." Sammy looked at Tim. "It's a shame. Because deep down, all those guys have good hearts."

29

"ARE YOU READY YOUNG LADY?" Dr. Hallahan was dressed in scrubs with a surgery cap covered in puppies.

Amelia nodded.

"Do you have any questions before we wheel you back?"

"Yeah. Do you have a dog?"

"Actually, I have two dogs. A Shiatzu and a Labrador. The lab is a therapy dog for my wife. Sometimes, like today, he's here at the hospital visiting patients." He smiled.

"Yes! Daddy, could I see him?"

Bernardo nodded. There was nothing he wouldn't do for this little girl. Mama J would call him blessed. And he guessed that was an excellent description. He and Marie were back together. His apprenticeship was in full swing, and he could now afford the rent and utilities. Let's just say it was a better environment than living at Joey's.

"Okay, young lady. Let's get this show on the road. You'll soon be a new creation."

Marie bent to kiss her forehead. Bernardo took her hand, the one without the IV, and gave it a kiss. The nurse wheeled her out, leaving Bernardo standing, with his arm around Marie.

"She's gonna be okay. We have to trust that. And Mama J said she was praying. That might be an ace in the hole." They walked down the hall, hands entwined.

"Let's get some coffee. We've got several hours to kill." Bernardo took her hand. Things were going so well. Then again, there was the issue of the heist money. If he came home with his share, Marie would know there had been monkey business. He couldn't afford to lose her again. At the same time, they could really use the money to cover Amelia's surgery. Should he come clean with her? If he was able to pay off Amelia's hospital bills, Marie was going to wonder how he could pay it.

He could make something up—like, insurance said they'd pay it all? The electrician's union had a special fund for families in need? Anxiety worked its way down to his stomach.

There was still time. He didn't need to worry about it now.

MAMA J and Ignacia sat at the computer, scrolling through the internet. She Googled *war in Ukraine*. The page populated with the history of the war, *Latest News and Updates, Is a ceasefire deal on the horizon*? She opened a map of Ukraine showing the captive areas.

"Brother Ben told me that the parents lived in Bucha, which was about fifty miles inland from the front line." Ignacia pointed to the map.

"Hmmm—does that mean they were safe from harm, or not? Fifty miles isn't that far away."

Next, she searched for flights from Ukraine to the U.S. The cheapest were from the Polish city of Rzeszow and landing in New York. Yes, they were the cheapest, but inexpensive was not cheap. Tickets were just over $1,000 apiece. Which, if multiplied by sixteen for both parents to come was a pretty big chunk of change. And then there would be the tickets for the kids as well. Where could they get that amount?

"What about passports? Do you think they even have them? Or is there an elevated price for them now?" Ignacia had just travelled to Rome and knew how much of a hassle getting passports and visas were in the U.S., let alone in a country at war.

"If they land in New York, how will you get them from New York to D.C.?" Ignacia asked.

"We could drive the kids in the van to New York. That might be easiest."

"Lord, I know nothing is impossible for you, but there are a lot of things that could interfere with this plan. The least of which is the cost."

JOEY SAT by the computer with G-Man, examining their cryptocurrencies. They had increased exponentially in the few weeks they had taken possession of them. Literally billions of dollars. Each new day seemed to bring fresh blessings. Rosie licked Joey's chin.

"How are you going to divide things up, Joey?"

Joey stared at the computer and bit his lower lip. He wasn't sure. His original plan was to divide things five ways, with the largest portion being his, of course. After all, he was the mastermind. But now, Slingshot was back in the concrete hotel, awaiting trial.

Joey had to take the blame for some of that. He was the one who had ordered Slingshot to kill Michael. And he had to say, he'd done a clean job of it. Just thinking back to the other night when he took down those three goons? The guy was good. He was a real asset. Maybe some of the money should go to pay for his defense.

And then there was Bernardo. He needs his share soon to pay for his daughter's surgery. That man deserved his share. He was instrumental in getting that weird thumb drive, which gave us the wealth they had now.

Don't forget G-Man—if he hadn't gotten into the computer, they wouldn't have the goods on top of the gold bars. And Smols played his part in the distraction. Let's face it—they each deserved their cut.

"Give me a few more days to think this through, G-Man."

BERNARDO WALKED down the hall reading a text.

"Look out, you nearly walked into this guy." Marie put her hand on Bernardo's arm.

A teen boy sat in a wheelchair and rolled the wheels backward to avoid Bernardo. He was clean, thick black hair, wearing a white hoodie and jeans.

"Oh, sorry man. I didn't mean to run into you."

"'Sokay. No worries." The boy brushed him off.

Bernardo and Marie took a few steps, then Bernardo turned back. "Wait. Do I know you?" He peered into the boy's dark eyes. "You look really familiar." Who did he remind him of?

The boy shrugged. "My name's Robbie, if that helps." They clasped hands, fingers locking in a firm grip, and pulled each other in. Their joined hands rose to shoulder height, forearms tightening for a moment before they released and Bernardo stepped back. He frowned and cocked his head. "Do you have an older brother?"

Robbie nodded.

"Named Joey?"

It was Robbie's turn to wear a quizzical look. He nodded slowly.

"And you were shot, weren't you." Bernardo looked at the wheelchair. Robbie nodded.

Dr. Hallahan interrupted them. He still wore scrubs and his puppies surgery cap, but they were no longer crisp and clean. He removed his glasses and hung them in the v of his shirt and smiled.

"Here you are. They're through with surgery. Amelia's in the recovery room."

Marie gripped Bernardo's arm. Her expression was a mixture of hope and fear.

"That's one sturdy little girl you've got there. The surgery was a success on all counts. It all went smoothly."

Marie and Bernardo shared an exhale. Relief spread from their heads to their toes, washing away the anxiety they had held onto for weeks.

"Can we see her?"

"Yes, of course. She's still drowsy, but you can go in. She'll be here for a few weeks, and you have permission to visit her at any time for as long as you'd like."

30

MAMA J FOLLOWED the girls into the house from morning mass. The focus was on taking care of the poor and downtrodden, about how much God cared for each one. She felt pretty good about where they were with that directive. They'd befriended the neighbors, and what a ride that had been. Hopefully, some of the sisters' trust and hope had rubbed off on them.

And then there were the kiddos. Of course, that was Brother Ben's mission, not the charge of the Sisters of Mercy, but they had the privilege of being with them.

And she was convinced that it was because of their prayers that they all came out unscathed.

"Someone's at the door," Agnes said. She pulled the heavy door open and looked up.

"Smols, hi! Come in out of the cold."

"I'll just be a minute. You all have been so nice to us, and well, we thought we could do something for you."

Mama J came up behind Agnes and welcomed him.

"We'd like to invite *you* for dinner tomorrow night, if that's okay. It'd be our New Year's gift to you."

"Well, now isn't that nice. We'd be honored. What could we bring?"

"You don't need to bring nuthin'. We've got it all planned out." Smols grinned like a little kid with a secret.

The next evening, the sisters trudged through the fresh layer of snow to the neighbor's house, bundled in scarves and warm coats. Squirt held a shovel in gloved hands and scooped snow off the sidewalk. He bowed and spread his outstretched arm towards the front door.

The weathered porch railing was adorned with twinkling lights and a wreath hung on the door. Mama J held her fist up, but before she could rap on the door, it opened.

"Come in, ladies. We're glad you could make it." Joey ushered them in. Before them were two folding tables, complete with white linen tablecloths and cloth napkins. Three white candles decorated the tables, with the flames glowing, giving a scent of lemon. The table held bits of sparkly New Year's confetti. The atmosphere felt clean and energizing, making Mama J have visions of fresh starts.

Behind the tables, Smols towered above them in the center, with Squirt and G-Man on either side, dressed in button-down shirts and ties.

Ignacia put her hands on her hips and shook her head. "You boys went all out, didn't you?"

They nodded. "You can probably see that we're missing two of us—Slingshot and Bernardo. He's celebrating with his wife and daughter at the hospital. And well, you already heard about Slingshot," Joey said. "Sit down."

Each of the men pulled folding chairs out for the ladies, seating them at every other chair. Mama J double- blinked. Would wonders never cease?

A man entered, dressed in black pants and a black, button-down shirt with Caruthers' Catering embroidered under the shoulder. He came from the kitchen carrying a large, round tray, with a steaming turkey. He set it in the center of the table, where eyes smiled at the heavenly scent. Squirt and G-Man brought out green beans and mashed potatoes.

"Would you like a glass of wine?" the server asked.

Agnes giggled. Other than for communion, she'd never drunk wine. She looked at Mama J, who nodded.

When they were all seated, the men sat, interspersed with the sisters. Mama J reached for Agnes and Joey's hands, who continued the circle and bowed their heads.

"In the name of the Father, Son and Holy Spirit. Dear Lord, we are so grateful for your love, which reached down from heaven to us. None of us deserves your tender care. Continue to bless these men, this delicious food, and us." Everyone joined in with "amen".

The server dished up their food and stood back.

As Mama J wondered how they could afford this, Joey, as if he could read her mind, said, "We came into some money and wanted to treat you guys. You've been awfully nice to us."

Smols held a roll in his hand. "And we felt really bad that the play got all messed up."

"We're sorry, Mama J. You guys should never have gotten mixed up in this." Squirt hung his head.

Mama J set her glass down. "Now Boys, I'm sure you couldn't have predicted things would have gone that way."

Joey glanced at G-Man.

"But we…" Squirt started.

Mama J waved off his reply. "Whatever happened, we don't need to know the details. What you have to understand is that God was in control. He worked out every detail. Both for you and for us."

Joey shook his head and became silent. How could this be? God isn't a real thing, is he? Besides, who's ever seen him? Then he pictured that little girl playing Mary and holding the baby. That baby was God, wasn't it. Someone *had* seen him.

The server took his plate. "Are you all ready for dessert, or should we wait?"

Smols patted his stomach. Irene groaned. "I'm so full."

The server nodded. "Just let me know when you're ready."

"Who's up for some ping pong?" Squirt pushed himself back from the table and stood.

Irene and Agnes followed Squirt and G-Man. They picked up the paddles, and within minutes the war was on. A few missed hits, chasing after balls, and sounds of laughter.

"It's good to hear them having fun. I'm not gonna lie, this week was a little stressful." Mama J folded her napkin.

"What's gonna happen to those kids?" Smols sopped up gravy with the remains of his roll.

"Funny you should ask. Ignacia and I were just hashing out a plan. I checked maps on the internet to see exactly where the parents lived. Then, I looked at flights to New York. They were less expensive than landing in D.C. But it's so expensive." Mama J frowned. "I just don't see how we could make it work. Brother Ben thinks it would do them both good to reconnect. Even if it was for a brief time."

Joey caught Smols' eye.

There were a whoop and a holler from the other room. Edith and Irene waved their hands in the air as they did a little dance. "Take that!" They laughed.

Squirt and G-Man tossed their paddles on the table and held their hands up in defeat.

"Hellooo...." Heads turned as Bernardo and Marie stepped into the room.

"What's going on here? Looks pretty fancy. And you didn't invite us?" Bernardo looked hurt.

"Gee, we thought you were at the hospital and were busy with Amelia. Sorry. How is she, anyways?" Joey said.

"Really good, everything went smooth as butter. She's resting." Bernardo helped Marie with her coat and threw it over the back of the couch.

"Come in. Sit down." Joey motioned to the couch. "Hey server, I think it's time for that pie, please. And bring a couple extra plates."

"We can't stay long. We left someone outside on the porch. It think you'll want to see who it is."

Joey cocked his head. "Yeah?" He followed Bernardo out to where a teen sat in a wheelchair.

"Gonna need some help to bring this guy up the steps."

"Joey?"

Joey started. Wait. He knew that voice. He removed his hat and took a step closer. His chest swelled, and his throat choked up. He flashed to that night. It had been brutal. The chaos of it all. An exploded car, gun shots, sirens. And when they were taking him away, put in handcuffs, Smols told him his brother had been shot. First shock—his brother should have been at home where he left him— then his head a jumbled mess trying to reason it out, his stomach ready to hurl.

"Robbie? No, it can't be." Joey took a step back. "I thought you were dead." He barely whispered.

Robbie nodded. "Could you help me in? It's really cold out here." He shivered.

Joey got on one side and with Smols on the other, hoisted him in and got him situated.

"What happened? No one told me." Joey held the bridge of his nose.

"I think they left me for dead. If you remember, there was a lot of chaos—gunshots, car races, sirens. When I followed you, I thought I could stay far enough behind to watch and make sure you were okay. But then, when I crouched behind the alley, a shot ricocheted, and it got me in the thigh. I went down."

The server came in with a tray of apple pie slices and handed them out.

"This looks super good." Robbie took a bite.

"Who found you?" Joey couldn't eat. He couldn't take his eyes off his little bro.

"The police. They put me in an ambulance and took me to the hospital."

"You haven't been in the hospital all that time, have you? That happened two years ago."

"No. The bullet shattered my femur, so the doctor put rods in there. I was doing okay, but it was bothering me, so they had to go in and repair it. They didn't want to send me home with no one to help me out." Robbie shrugged.

Joey got down on his knees and put his hands on Robbie's cheeks. He let his head fall onto Robbie's lap, where Robbie ran his hands through his older brother's hair.

"I am so, so sorry. That should never have involved you." He sat up and turned to Mama J. "My life choices should never have involved you either." He shook his head.

"Joey, it's okay. I'm going to be able to walk. I'll need physical therapy, but I'm okay. Don't worry about it."

"We've got room for you here. If you're willing, that is."

Robbie reached out and wrapped his arms around Joey's neck, holding tight as if he could slip away from him again.

31

BROTHER BEN SAT in an armchair next to the fireplace. Orange and yellow flames danced on the logs, radiating a welcome heat. Mama J set her legs on a footrest and made herself comfortable on the couch. The only sound was the crackle of the fire.

"This is nice. A respite from the convent. Not to say that I don't enjoy the hubbub of the girls and keeping our hands and minds busy. But it's nice to have a few moments of quiet and good company."

"Agreed. The kids are all nestled in their beds."

"Yeah, it went surprisingly without a hitch."

Ben lifted the tea cozy from a hot teapot. He poured two cups and handed one to Joanna.

She nodded a thanks and wrapped her hands around the warm cup. "There's just the matter of that last gift I keep rolling around in my head."

Ben nodded. "I've spent a fair amount of time exploring all the options. I spoke with the head of the organization that sent the kids here originally. They thought it was a wonderful idea. There are spots in Ukraine that seem to be safe for the time being. First, we would have to notify the parents of the possibility."

Mama J sat up straighter. "That must be a God thing—the timing." She nodded her head slowly, thinking. "What would be the logistics?"

"The organization would procure train tickets for the parents to Romania, where they would then take a plane to New York City—those are the cheapest tickets." Ben straightened a lap quilt over his knees and took a sip of tea.

"So, we'd need to get the kids from here to meet them there? Or would the parents come here?"

"I suppose it would be cheapest if the kids were to meet them in New York and they could fly them back." Ben picked up a Rubik's Cube from the end table and started twisting it.

"There would be fewer accommodations to plan for, for sure."

"I spoke with the provincial superior in New York, and he said they could all stay at the abbey for as long as they needed."

Mama J nodded. This was all coming together nicely. Now, about how to pay for it.

"How ya doing, Baby?" Bernardo held Marie's hand as they walked into Amelia's hospital room.

"Daddy! Mama!" A smile lit her face, and she hugged the large teddy bear by her side. She was still hooked to an IV—the clear liquid in the bag dripping slowly to her veins.

The nurse entered, wheeling a cart for lab work.

"I need to do a few draws to make sure everything is up to snuff. Amelia, I just need to do a couple of tests for your blood lactate and a coagulation test. No pokes this time." She smiled and set the tray with alcohol wipes, labeled tubes and syringes.

She turned the clamp on the tubing to stop the flow of fluids.

Amelia allowed the nurse to take her hand as she removed the alcohol wipe from the package and cleaned the access port. The faint smell surrounded them. In a swift move, the nurse twisted the syringe onto the port with a click and slowly pulled back on the plunger.

"Look, Daddy, that red stuff is my blood. Isn't it pretty?"

Bernardo tried to smile but looked away. Blood was never in his comfort zone.

"All done. We'll have the results for coagulation and ABG, which measures oxygen levels, back soon. You can check at the nurse's station before you go. This young lady is doing surprisingly well. If this continues, I think the doctor will release her at the end of the week.

"You mean I could go home?"

"That's right." She gathered the tray and wheeled it out.

Marie straightened her sheet and fluffed her pillow. "What do you miss most?"

Amelia looked at the ceiling. "Umm, being able to run and jump."

"It will still be a while before you can do that, but it's something to look forward to, for sure."

"I'm going to get coffee and something to eat. What can I bring you?" Bernardo looked from Amelia to Marie.

"I want ice cream!"

Marie smiled. "I'll take coffee and a pastry, please."

Bernardo nodded and stepped into the hall. He found the elevator and touched the 2nd floor button. He'd go to the food court after he talked to someone in the finance office.

"Hey, my names Bernardo Sanchez, and my daughter Amelia has been here for three weeks. I wanted to check and see how much I might owe for her surgery and stay." He swallowed hard. This had to be in multiples of thousands.

A woman in a cubicle waved him over. "Have a seat. Let's see what we can find out."

She took his information and scrolled through her computer.

Bernardo's knee tapped up and down.

"It looks here like you're not going to owe anything."

Bernardo frowned. How was that possible?

"What? That's not possible."

She peered more closely at her computer and scrolled down more.

"No, that's right. Apparently, an anonymous donor paid for the surgery with the note that any other follow-ups would be covered as well." She looked up and grinned.

Bernardo stood dazed.

"Have a nice day!"

THE AIR WAS crisp and clear—the sun forming sparkling diamonds on the remaining snow. It was the perfect day for a field trip to the Natural History Museum and a special surprise.

Agnes and Irene helped the kids into their warm jackets and handed them each a backpack filled with snacks of crackers and peanut butter, Oreos, and juice boxes. She also included small notepads and a few colored pens to doodle on in the van if they got bored.

Ignacia filled a backpack with band aids, lotions, wet wipes, tweezers and other emergency supplies. Hopefully, they wouldn't need them, but it never hurt to be prepared.

Brother Ben pulled the fifteen-passenger van in front of the gate and slid the door open. He couldn't wait to see the kids' faces of awe when they stood beside giant dinosaurs and woolly mammoths.

"Load up, kiddos." They filed in one by one, snapped their seatbelts and took off with Agnes in the front seat and Mama J, Irene, Ignacia, and Edith following close behind in their van. It didn't take long to find a place to park by the metro stop, and they all bailed out.

"Where are we?" Olena asked.

"We're close to the National Mall. We'll take the metro to the museum." Mama J paired each kid with an adult, with Bohdan holding Vova's hand and Mykita and Liliya holding hands.

"Stay with your partners. We don't want to lose any of you." Mama J counted heads stopping at Ivan's. No, she didn't want to lose Ivan again.

They hustled down the steep steps and waited as the kachunk kachunk of the metro came down the track. The doors slid open, and people piled out. Mama J counted heads again and led the way, and Brother Ben took up the rear.

A few stops later, they arrived.

"We're at the National Mall, where the Natural History Museum is. We get to see dinosaurs and all sorts of animals. You'll love it!" Edith said.

"Dinosaurs? Yay!" Vova jumped up and down.

They counted all ten steps as they climbed the stairs. Bohdan stopped and bent over, taking in a huge breath.

Once inside, they stopped at an enormous, grey elephant—it's trunk in the air. If this was all they saw today, it would have been worth coming here. Their jaws dropped as their eyes travelled to the gigantic ears and ivory tusks.

"What are those?" Bohdan pointed at the dinosaur skeletons.

"Bones. That's what's inside of you." Taras pointed.

"In me?"

"In all of us." Taras showed him how to feel his ribs.

Mama J smiled and met Brother Ben's gaze. Was that a hint

of sadness? Maybe. She had to admit that she felt a bit of it as well.

A few hours later after seeing the bison, porcupines, lions and hundreds of birds, Ben checked the time. He gathered them onto a long bench.

"Anyone hungry?"

"Yes, I'm so hungry I could eat a dinosaur!" Ivan said.

"Okay, we're close to the cafeteria. When we get there, you can choose whatever you want to eat. This is a special day." He led them through the smorgasbord and sat them at the tables. Surprisingly, they carried their trays successfully with no spills.

Ben whispered to Mama J. "I'll be back." He nodded his head towards the entrance.

She replied with a nod. Her shoulders raised, and she closed her eyes and let out a long breath.

32

THERE WERE no mistaking the parents. Each dressed in clothing intricately embroidered. Fathers stood tall, arms protectively around their wives, eyes searching the crowd.

Brother Ben strode toward them—their eyes soon connected across the room. Mothers turned to their spouses and pointed.

"You're here!" Ben beamed. "Your children are eating lunch. They have no idea that you are here."

One mother let tears stream down her cheeks.

"You've had a long trip and a lot of logistics to manage. Let's not delay a second longer."

A collective breath was heard as they followed Ben, not seeing the elephant, or the skeletons. All that could wait. There was only one goal in their minds.

When they arrived at the cafeteria, they stood momentarily and searched the room, then ran towards their children.

"Mama? Tato?" A look of complete surprise erupted on the children' faces. The children leapt from their seats and ran into the embrace of their parents.

Ben stood by Mama J and shook his head. He couldn't stop

grinning. If this wasn't a miraculous act of God, he didn't know what was.

THE BOYS and their parents stayed the night at Hope House, and the girls and their parents stayed at the convent with the sisters.

Agnes and Irene had prepared a large breakfast of fresh scrambled eggs, bacon, scones and hot cocoa. As they ate, Mama J excused herself for a phone call.

"Yes? Really? How dreadful." She went to her office and shut the door. "You said the pilot is in the hospital? How long will he be there?" She shook her head and sat down.

"At least a week? Oh, that's not going to work. They need to get back to Ukraine."

Mama J had an idea. But would it work? She had let her license expire years ago. She lifted her eyes to the Lord. Sensing a nod, she spoke. "I was a jet pilot years ago. It might be possible for me to fly them home."

She mumbled, "Are you sure about this, Lord?"

BY THE NEXT MORNING, all suitcases were loaded with clothes, gifts, food and books. They stood at the terminal, ready to board the jet. Ben had kept their passports in a safe and handed them to the parents. He was no longer in charge of them. This day was bittersweet. He would miss their voices and caring for them. He would even miss their arguments and messes. Who knew what would be next. God always had something in mind. He nodded, placed his palms together and lifted his hands to the sky.

Mama J stood beside him. It had been a miracle, really.

"Funny how God would use a talent from twenty years ago to

fulfill his purpose," she said. "He just seems to layer things in our lives."

"That he does. And answers prayers."

She nodded.

Mama J reflected on the extraordinary circumstances that had unfolded.

"I mean, who but God would have arranged for someone to donate money anonymously with the designation of a private jet from and to Ukraine? He never ceases to amaze me."

The sense of wonder at how things had come together was shared by Ben. The anonymous donation, specifically earmarked for their journey, was nothing short of miraculous. Every detail had been carefully orchestrated, re-affirming their belief in divine intervention.

Mama J gave Ben a two-fingered salute.

"Well, Captain, we'll see you soon. Safe travels!"

FOR WHERE YOUR TREASURE IS, *there will your heart be also.*
Matthew 6:21

AFTERWORD

I could never have anticipated how much fun this story was so fun to write. When God dropped the title into my head, I said, "Really?"

Then I shrugged my shoulders, because so far, everything he's told me to do has turned out to either be fun, or richly rewarding.

When I shared my new venture with my daughter, the nun, she was appalled. Then she laughed and turned to the sister next to her.

"Okay. Tell her what happened."

That story became the first chapter.

Then my imagination went wild. Who was Bunny Slippers and what was his story? Why would he need to steal a van?

That morphed into the ex-cons, neighbors to the sisters.

And of course there had to be a dead body, right?

I hope you enjoyed reading this as much as I did writing it.

If so, I would love if you would write a quick review.

Here are some tips:

Essential elements to include:

Start with the basics - title, author, and maybe a one-sentence description of what kind of book it is. Then give your overall impression before diving into details. This helps readers know right away if they should keep reading your review.

Questions to guide your writing:

For the story itself, you might ask: What's the book about at its core? What happens, and does the plot keep you engaged? Are there twists or does it follow a predictable path? Does the pacing work?

For characters, consider: Who are the main characters and what makes them interesting (or not)? Do they feel real and three-dimensional? Do you care what happens to them? Do they change or grow?

For setting, think about: Where and when does the story take place? Does the world-building feel immersive? Is the setting just a backdrop or does it shape the story?

Other useful angles:

What's the writing style like - lyrical, straightforward, funny, dense? What themes or ideas does the book explore? How did it make you feel? Who would enjoy this book, and who might not? How does it compare to similar books or the author's other work?

The most important part: Be honest and specific. Instead of saying "the characters were great," explain what made them memorable. Give examples when you can, but avoid major spoilers - or at least warn readers first.

A good review doesn't need to cover all of these areas. Focus on what stood out to you most, whether positive or negative. Your authentic reaction is what makes a review valuable.

ACKNOWLEDGMENTS

A special thank you to my son Kyle Rea, whose insider knowledge about cryptocurrency gave me accurate details to include.

And my son Jed Johnson, whose ideas gave me so many shenanigans and ideas to work with.

I would also like to acknowledge Shawn Campbell, who gave invaluable input to help make this story as funny as possible.

My artistic daughter, Sara Rea, helped refine the design for the cover.

My daughter, Sister Mercy, whose insight into nun life was invaluable.

I truly couldn't have written this without their help.

ABOUT THE AUTHOR

Jan Johnson has been writing for most of her life. It began with a space story that she wrote and her dad bound, giving her the confidence to call herself an author.

Jan lives on a sheep farm on the coast of Oregon with her husband Ed. Don't mistake living on a farm as meaning she likes animals. Well, she actually does- from a distance.

She's passionate about building relationships, meeting new people and hearing their stories. You know what they say-Love God, love people.

When she isn't writing, starting something new, or podcasting, she catches up with her ten children, who are scattered hither and yon.

This is Jan's seventh book.